To

much Love!

The Hip-Hop Series
Word Works by, for and in the Language of
the New Urban Generation

Www.PenknifePress.Com

One
Dead
Activist

One Dead Activist
A David Price Mystery
by
Tony Lindsay

Penknife Press   Chicago, Illinois

Copyright © 2022 by Tony Lindsay
All rights reserved under International and Pan-American Copyright Conventions.
Published in the United States of America by Penknife Press, Ltd., Chicago, Illinois.

ISBN 978-1-59997-036-3

Library of Congress Control Number: 2022950426

Manufactured in the United States of America

Acknowledgments

A heartfelt thank you to my close readers: Roy Mock and Florine Weston.

For my mother,
Sadie B. Davis

Love you, mama.

Chapter One

Summer 2018

It was a clear blue-sky day, and the temperature was in the low eighties with a northern breeze. It was a perfect day for sitting on the front porch, but Ricky Brown and I weren't sitting on porch steps; instead, we were standing in front of Chicago's police headquarters with about thirty other people. There was a line of about twenty armed police officers behind our protesting group, and there were ten more officers to our left and another ten to our right. They had formed a horseshoe around our group.

Five minutes earlier, it was only us, the protesters; the police presence was sudden, and the officers in blue didn't make anyone in our group feel safe, but the news media was there, and some people in our group had camera phones. If the police had tried anything, they would have been recorded.

I'd chambered a round in my Berretta .380 before I got out of the car, and I said a prayer when I saw the police lining up. That was all I could do. I blew out a long breath and returned my attention to the young man standing on a blue milk crate in the doorway of police headquarters.

He was dressed in knee length blue jean shorts, brown closed toe sandals, and a green army fatigue patterned t-shirt. In his hand was a silver and orange bullhorn. It was only July, but four young Black men had been shot and killed by Chicago police. "What I am telling you is the truth." The young activist yelled into the bullhorn. His head was shaved bald, and he had a black ankh tattooed on the crown of his Milk Dud-brown head. "Africans fought against the Dutch, the Portuguese, the French, the Spanish, and the British. Africans didn't just let invaders come onto the continent and take people. There were battles: barracoons were attacked, ships were sunk, and the Senegal River turned red with the blood of invaders."

He wiped the sweat from his brow with the back of his hand, and he started shaking his head no. "Africans did not stand still and passively accept the abduction of their people, nor were the captured docile; history is littered with shipboard revolts and sunken slave ships that never left port because of Africans fighting for their lives.

"We have never been a people who took injustice. We have always fought back." He became silent and looked over the crowd. He started nodding his head yes and said, "Africans fought throughout the Caribbean; plantations were burned to the ground. Slavers were slain from Haiti to Virginia. Do not ever believe that we are not warriors. Nat Turner showed us that, Dorie Miller showed us that. We are not weak people, and we fight against injustice. Medgar Evers showed us that." His bald head lowered as if he was in prayer, and again he shook it to the negative. "No...no...we are not docile people; Watts showed us that, Huey P. Newton showed us that,

Malcolm showed us that, and Fred Hampton showed us that. We don't sit still. And if this city thinks police violence is acceptable to us, we are here to tell them different! It will not be tolerated, not...by...us!"

The kid raised his black-gloved right fist and was pounding the air with each word establishing the beat: "Not... by... us! Not... by... us! Not... by... us!"

The protestors erupted with his chant.

"Not...by...us! Not...by...us! Not...by...us!"

And without consciously realizing it, I was chanting too. "Not... by... us! Not... by... us!" And so was my friend, Ricky Brown, "Not... by... us! Not... by... us! Not... by... us!"

*

The news cameras had caught the mood of the morning, and the effectiveness of the kid activating the crowd. Ricky and I were grinning standing in my living room looking at the playback on the mid-day news.

The kid was the epitome of the term, "activist." An enthusiast had placed a flyer under my windshield wiper during the protest. *Chicago's Homegrown Activist* was the heading above the kid's picture.

"People like dis kid. Dey callin' him da next Malcolm," Ricky said, standing in front of my wall-mounted fifty-inch television. He walked from the television to the couch and dropped his mass down. Then, he tossed his keys on the coffee table. I'd asked him to stop doing both of those actions. Ricky Brown weighed close to four hundred pounds, and when he just dropped down on a piece of furniture, it took a toll. My couch and the matching love seat weren't three months old, so they were still new to me, and each time he dropped down on the couch, I cringed.

I placed a bamboo mat across the length of my antique coffee table because he tossed his keys on the table whenever he dropped his fat ass down on my couch. To save myself frustration and to add life to our forty plus year friendship, I covered the coffee table with a decorative bamboo mat, and I had additional support added to the frame of my new black leather couch because I really didn't know if Ricky's knees or gravity would allow him to sit instead of drop. I gave my friend the benefit of the doubt.

My dog Sonny, a white and brindle Johnson American Bulldog, did not like Ricky. When he entered the house, Sonny went into guard mode and followed him step for step. That afternoon when Ricky dropped down on the couch, Sonny sat down right in front of him. Ricky noticed it and said, "Man, I been knowin' dis mut fo' three years since he was puppy."

Ricky looked into Sonny his face and asked, "When he gonna stop treatin' me like a stranger? I heard you tell him 'friend' a couple of hundred times, but er time I come in here, he paces my damn steps. What's up wid dat?"

I started to mention me telling him about tossing his keys on my coffee table a hundred times, but I didn't. Sonny is a beautiful dog, but he is incredibly stubborn. He has the traditional brindle spot covering half his face and his hind quarter. I looked down at him and watched him go from sitting and watching Ricky to laying down and watching Ricky.

Sonny only trusted a handful of people: my son Chester, Wendy the coffee shop owner, and my ex-wife who is my current girlfriend. He watched everyone else that got close to me including Ricky.

"The dog has a brain of his own, Ricky. He's a trained guard dog. He is only doing what he was trained to do." I sat down in my recliner and asked, "So, you really think the kid is the next Malcolm? That would make him quite the activist." I held up the flyer for emphasis.

My friend looked from my dog to me as he sat back into the couch. After the protest at police headquarters, we went to the barbershop. Ricky got his short afro trimmed with scissors, and he insisted on a straight razor lining, so his cut looked fresh.

He had been going to the beauty shop and getting his hair done since our teens; we both used to get our hair relaxed. I stopped wearing the style when I went to college, but Ricky didn't stop until last year when the beautician informed that he'd gotten too big for her salon chairs. She told him she would have to come to his home to do his hair. Ricky was insulted, so he started going to the barber shop with me. I go to the barber to get my bread trimmed and lined up. I shave my own head bald.

"Ya know, I saw dat word on da flyer, and I heard people callin' him dat, but what do dey mean... activist?"

Ricky and I went to the same college; he didn't graduate, but he took the same African American Studies classes I did. We, most of the Black students, took the classes to improve our Black consciousness and in my case to save my GPA. I got all A's in the African American Studies classes because I did the work; the topics interested me. Ricky spoke as if he never went to college, but he did... for two years, and he earned better grades than me.

"Well, from my understanding, the term activist refers to a person who sacrifices self-interest for the betterment of their community, a person who puts forward efforts to uplift others, people like Malcolm X, Sojourner Truth, Dr. King, and Harriet Tubman. Folks who put their communities first."

He nodded his big brown head in the affirmative and said, "Mmph, well I don't know if da young brotha is a Harriet Tubman, but he givin' da Chicago police and da mayor's office hell-of-a headaches. You see him on da news every couple of days protestin' somethin', mostly dese police shootin's."

The young activist was all over the television and in the papers almost daily.

"Chester said he and others tried to talk him into running for mayor, but the kid told them he was an activist, not a politician." The news broadcast on the television ended and a bank commercial was playing offering no money down financing for homes.

"How do Chester know da young rebel?"

Sonny yawned and licked his chops while still watching Ricky.

"They went to the same high school, and they went away to college together."

"Do you know his people?" Ricky asked, looking across the room to my bar.

"Nope, and I never met him. Chester said the young activist was raised in different foster homes, but a group of Black male social workers kept him in the same schools and took an interest in his college education, and the activist credits them for keeping him on right path." I picked up the remote from the lamp table and cut the television off.

"Da kid got lucky."

A whiff of the Lavender Woods potpourri passed my nose and made me smile. The crockpot mixture behind the bar was working just fine.

"Chester says that group of social workers has done the same for dozens of kids in the city." I pushed back in my recliner and the footrest extended. I was ready for my Saturday afternoon nap; it was getting to be time for Ricky to leave.

He got up from the couch and went over to the bar and poured himself a double shot of Hennessy VSOP Cognac in one of my crystal snifters; he brought me the Cognac for Christmas. Sonny watched him, but he didn't stand. Ricky came back to the couch sat heavily and said, "Tina joined the high school reunion committee with Wifey."

Those words made me push the leg rest down and sit up straight in the recliner. Wifey was Martha, Ricky's wife for thirty plus years, and Tina was a woman he dated before he was married. For clarification, I asked him, "Tina, from high school, the dentist's wife? The woman you are...?"

"Yep" was his answer.

Ricky and Tina had been involved in a decades-long, on-again-off-again extramarital affair. One I have been annoyed with for most of its existence. I looked over to my bar and said, "Damn, that could be a little messy." I got up and walked over to the bar, poured myself a shot of Cognac in a snifter, and returned to my comfy chair.

He shook his head no. "Nope, not really, we been careful all dese years; ain't nothin' gonna change."

Ricky had dated Tina first, but he didn't marry her. He dated Martha for what seemed like a couple of days and married her. When Tina heard he was getting married, she shot out his car windows a week before the wedding, and she promised to show up at the wedding dressed in black with her wicked ass girlfriends. Ricky believed her, so he had her kidnapped the day before the wedding and held for three days.

When Ricky's kidnappers released her, Tina came to see to me, and told me to tell Ricky to call her the day he came back from the honeymoon. I did, and he did call her, and she kept seeing him romantically after he married Martha. It was Ricky who introduced Tina to Dr. Gates, our dentist. She married the dentist, but she never stopped seeing Ricky, and Ricky stayed a patient of Dr. Gates. I sat in my comfy chair just looking at him.

"What?" He drained his glass.

"All these years, haven't you ever been a little worried when you are laying back in his dentist chair?"

He nodded his fat clumpy head in the affirmative. "Shit, a lot worried, I don't eva go widout my pistol, but if I stop seein' him dat might bring suspicion down on Tina. All she eva told him was we was high school friends."

I stopped going to Dr. Gates when Ricky told me he and Tina were kicking it again. "Damn." I turned my drink up.

"So dis da situation. Wifey invited Tina and her family over fo' Sunday dinner."

He was looking at me like I was going to say something. All I had was "Damn."

He exhaled and looked down at Sonny. "Yeah, I know, right. I was hopin' you would come on ova too."

I felt my eyebrows raise all the up. "Me?" Oh, *hell no* was my thought. "Why you need me?" The situation sounded stressful, very stressful, and I was not one to volunteer for stress. He didn't look at me with the request which was his way. He never looked at me when he was asking a favor. His gaze was on the top of Sonny's head.

"I need ya to help me wid talkin' to dem, shit... him mostly. And I don't really know what's up wid Tina, I was wid her two days ago, and she didn't say nothin' about join' the committee, meetin' wid Wifey, or comin' over Sunday fo' dinner."

More stress, nothing about the situation seemed inviting.

"Damn," I said again. My logical brain was screaming *hell no - don't go*, but my friendship loyal heart asked him, "What time?"

He looked up from Sonny and a big grin appeared across his fat face. "Eight o'clock, bro."

We had been friends for forty-plus years, and that was not first stressed-filled situation he put me in, and it wouldn't be the last. I looked over to my bar considering another shot.

"Ok, what should I bring?"

"Get one of dem Entenmann's Louisiana crunch cakes."

He needed the carbs from a crunch cake like he needed another hole in the head. I watched my carb intake, and there was sit up board on the side on my bed. When I woke up, it was bathroom then the sit-up board. Sit-ups started every day of my life, and my stomach was flat. I did two hundred pushups and squats throughout the day which was why my pecs and thighs were toned. I had an exercise room in the basement with a stationary bike, weight bench, and dumbbells, all of which I used daily because being overweight was not going to be the cause of my death. My mouth was not going to kill me.

"I don't think they come sugar free."

"Fuck ya, I didn't ask ya to get a sugar free one." My big friend laughed, grabbed his keys from the coffee table, rocked forward a couple times, and finally stood with a lengthy exhale.

"Ima go on and get outta here, so ya can take yo' old man nap."

Sonny stood with him.

"Dis fuckin' mutt."

Ricky walked to the front door with Sonny beside him.

Chapter Two

I woke to my phone ringing and vibrating on my chest. I had become a sound sleeper while napping, and placing the phone on my chest stopped me from missing business. Carol, my business partner, stopped working on Saturdays about seven years ago, so office calls came to my cell. I grabbed the phone and blinked my eyes open. The screen of the phone read Chester Price. My son was calling me. I tapped the phone on the screen.

"Hey Dad."

I sat up in the chair lowering my legs. "What's up, Son? Your uncle and I went to see your activist friend. He knows how to move a crowd. I'll give him that much."

Chester chuckled. "Yeah, he's a solid brother. Actually... he is why I am calling you." Chester's lowered tone of voice told me he was worried. "He's been getting some serious threats, and we have decided it is time to get some professional help, and of course I thought of you."

The boy, no... the young man, my son, made me smile. I was the owner of Epsilon Protection, a bodyguard service.

"Ok, so what do you mean serious threats?"

"Phone calls threatening his life."

"Ok, and who is the 'we'?"

"His friends. His close circle. You know, the people that have his back."

"Interesting. Does the group have a name?"

"Not really, Dad. It is just us; most of us have been friends since high school."

"When did the calls start?"

"Honestly, he has always gotten some crazy calls; *stay in your place, nigga calls* – we call them, but the calls that have us concerned are recent, and they are making a demand."

"A demand?"

"Yes sir, and we'd rather discuss it face-to-face. Are you free to meet this evening?"

"What time?"

"We were hoping for eight tonight?"

"Where?"

"At Wilson's place, 7419 S. Halsted. He lives above a store, a used appliance store. Norton is on the bell."

My son wanted to hire me. A big grin had spread across my face.

"Ok, see you there, Son."

I disconnected the call and looked over at Sonny. He was sitting up waiting and slightly smiling.

A walk usually followed my Saturday afternoon naps, and he liked the Dan Ryan Woods Forest preserve. I allowed him to run free there because he was trained well enough for that freedom. I checked my watch; it read 6:05, Jul. 17, 2018. There was time to drive him to the forest preserve, let him run, and return home.

"Ok, Sonny, let's go."

He stood, wagged his tail maybe two or three times, and waited for me to walk to the door. He was not an overly excitable dog.

*

I was standing at the top of the tobogganing hill in the evening sun watching Sonny chasing the orange rubber ball I threw. He'd break out after the orange ball and retrieve it before it could bounce twice in the grassy knoll of the small valley. He blazed through the grass bringing the ball back to me. He played hard, but if a stranger approached, he instantly stopped playing and went into guard mode.

Before Sonny, I had two Dobermans: Yin and Yang. I had them for nine years, and they died six months apart from each other. I hadn't thought about getting another dog, but I was in Ogden Park, and I saw a little old lady in her late seventies or early eighties walking a huge bulldog with no leash. The dog looked like a giant pit bull with big ears. I didn't know the breed, so I stopped the old lady with a question.

"What kind of dog is that? I have never seen a pit that tall."

She stopped walking and said, "Oh, Jackie is not a pit; she is a Johnson American Bulldog, and she is the best dog I have ever had. Aren't you, girl?"

Jackie's gaze stayed on me. The huge animal didn't growl, she simply watched me.

Looking closer at the dog, I saw her swollen tits hanging.

"Sit, Jackie," the old lady commanded. The dog sat, but I was still the target of her attention. She impressed me.

"She just had a litter of five puppies. Four have been spoken for, and I have three inquiries into the fifth. Would you like to see him?"

I had no plans on getting a puppy, but looking at the mother watching me, I heard myself saying, "yes."

Even as a puppy, Sonny was reserved. He came to the edge of the dog gate and looked up at me. He wagged his puppy tail two or three times then he sat down and puppy barked for me to pick him. When I picked him up, he didn't lick me; he just laid his head on my chest and went to sleep. I paid the old lady $1500 for Sonny. That was the most I ever paid for a dog.

Something stopped Sonny from chasing the orange ball. He stood statue still at the bottom of the grassy hill and looked to the trees. Two ragged coyotes emerged from the woods with ears lowered, baring teeth; neither had the height or the girth of Sonny, but it was two of them. I drew my pistol from under my Walter Payton Bears' jersey and made it down the hill.

As the coyotes approached, Sonny's left hind leg began kicking up grass. That move confused the coyotes. They stopped approaching. Sonny attention was on the leader, and his attack was swift. The roles of predator and prey switched. He had the larger of the two coyotes by the neck, and he flung the coyote to ground with such force that the other coyote cowered back. I was certain the coyote in Sonny's mouth had a broken neck.

The other coyote advanced and withdrew a couple of times before finally deciding to retreat into the woods. Sonny dropped the coyote carcass from his mouth. He stood over it not sure of what to do next; his primitive canine instinct only went so far. Food for him came from cellophane pouches, tin cans, and paper sacks, and the meals were served in a bowl with his name on it. I whistled, and Sonny galloped to me.

The trainer and the vet had advised me against letting him kill. The first time Sonny killed, he was barely nine months old, and a German Shepard attacked him at a park. The Shepard's owner took me to court, but Sonny's age caused the judge to rule in our favor. Sonny's second kill was an armed carjacker.

*

Sonny and I were at my friend Wendy's coffee and doughnut shop on 63rd and Bishop. Skinny, knocked kneed Wendy was one of three girls that played on the teen softball team I coached. She was a hell of a shortstop, and she was only nineteen when she opened the coffee shop five years ago. I was one of her initial investors; she opened the shop with community investors only, so people in the 'hood took pride in the business. I was at the shop Monday through Friday at crack of dawn, and I was always one of the first customers at her door.

That morning, I was the first, so I had parked right in front of the shop. I let Sonny out of the car, and he

obediently sat outside the shop door waiting for me, or…
for Wendy to bring him out a plain doughnut and talk
baby talk to him while he scarfed it down. When he was a
little puppy, I would bring him into her shop in my arms.
He and Wendy became fast friends. She told me, "I am a
cat person, but your puppy has charm." She has been
feeding him plain doughnuts and baby talking him since
day one.

The morning of the attempted carjacking, I had exited
the shop when a gunman came up behind me and pressed
his pistol against the base of my skull. I had a coffee in
one hand and two bagged doughnuts in the other.

"Give me the keys," the carjacker ordered in a scratchy
whisper. He smelled like piss and shit. Before I could
answer or move, I heard him scream, "Oh fuck!"

I dropped to a squatted position turning on my heels
to avoid his pistol's discharge. Moving away, I saw Sonny
had taken the gunman down by tearing half of his thigh
from the bone. I could see his thigh bones and the
pumping blood. Once the gunman was on the ground,
Sonny pounced on his chest and ripped open his throat.

I called Sonny to heel, and he instantly complied, but
there was no way the carjacker was alive. It happened in
seconds, and I had to think fast. Waiting for the police
and explaining what happened was a no-win situation for
Sonny. The law required a dog that killed to be put down
immediately without exception.

I looked up and down the street and saw no witnesses.
The carjacker was dead, and Sonny was at my side

sniffing at the doughnut bag which I was somehow still holding. I looked to the coffee shop door and saw no one. So, me and my dog got into the BMW I had at that time... and left.

The next morning, I went to shop without Sonny, and Wendy told me all about the police finding a known carjacker that had been mauled to death, "right in front of my door."

She and I were standing at the register when she said, "The police figured somebody he'd jacked in the past caught up with him. I told them I didn't see a thing which was true. I didn't." She put her brown paper bag eyes on me earnestly and continued with, "But if I was you, I would keep Sonny at home for a week or two just in case. And I put him an extra plain doughnut in the bag." Wendy got very nice Christmas gifts from me every year. Sonny functioned as a tool in my business, and much like my pistols, he had to be deadly.

    *

As soon as we entered the house, my cell phone started ringing and vibrating in my pocket. It was Regina, my ex-wife and current girlfriend calling, and I felt myself smiling. Sonny went to his meal bowl, and I answered the phone while walking into the kitchen pantry.

"Hey baby."

"Hey D. What are you doing?"

"About to feed the dog, then I need to shower and change clothes because I have a client meeting in a half an hour with your son." Saying that reminded me to call my business partner, Carol. Having her at initial client meetings had become a necessity. She possessed an eye for bullshit that slipped beyond my awareness.

"Really. I just spoke to Chester, and he didn't mention it. Humph?" The reporter in my ex-wife seeped out in that comment. Chester not telling her we were meeting got her curious, and she paused before saying, "Well, I am calling because I was feeling like going to the movies and getting a nice catfish dinner."

I was thinking about going to see *Superfly*, but I knew she was thinking *The Hate U Give*. "Were you now? Catfish, huh?" She'd interviewed the author of the novel a couple of months prior, so I knew she wanted to see the film.

"I was. And since my man spoils me and gives me what I want, I was calling to see what showtime I should pick."

My ex-wife and I started dating three months ago, after her mother's funeral. We'd both spent the night of the funeral at Chester's; he was close to his grandmother, and her death hurt him. The next morning, the two of us, Regina and I, went to breakfast. She started crying about her mother, and I put my arm around her for comfort.

In my defense, it was the first time we had embraced so closely in over a decade. Yes, I understood her mother had died six days ago, and I was fully aware that the only reason her head against my chest was because she was grieving the loss of her mother, but... my jones got hard, rock hard, strain the cloth on my pants hard.

I prayed to God... begging Him to not let her notice. But, while she was crying, her hand fell into my lap and landed right on top of my jones. I thought she was going to sit erect and slap me. Instead, she grabbed ahold of my erect jones while she wept with her head against my chest.

That morning at my place, not Chester's, we fucked liked newlyweds. Over twenty years had passed since we enjoyed each other's body. I thought she would want gentle holding and tenderness. I thought wrong. She rode me like a hobby horse and demanded hard doggy style sex which I happily supplied.

"What are our choices?" I asked my ex-wife-girlfriend. The phone was between my head and shoulder as I poured Sonny's food from a big bag. With the bowl full, he went at it. I folded the bag closed and returned it to the floor of the pantry. I walked to the kitchen table and sat looking out the window over the maple trees to the sky; dusk had come to the city.

"Well, your meeting will probably go at least a half hour, so that leaves us 9:15, or 9:45."

"And what are we going to see?"

"I was thinking *The Hate U Give*?"

I heard the excitement in her voice.

"Ok, let's go with 19:45 that way we can get the fish at JJ's and see the movie."

"See, that's why I love you, David Price. See you in a little while," and she hung up.

Her words jolted me.

Regina saying "see that's why I love you" caused me to hold the phone to my ear without hanging it up. I heard the call disconnect before I lowered the phone.

Yes, we had been going out for three months, but she never said, "I love you." I'd whispered the words in her ear while making love, and I ended most of our phone conversations with them, but I really didn't expect her to return the "I love you" words. Her actions showed me she cared.

We were fucking two to three times a week, and we were not living in the same place. Us getting together that often, took an effort of both our parts. She was busy and so was I, but we made time to see each other, and ninety-five percent of the time when we saw each other, we fucked. Me telling her "I love you" came easy for me because it was true. I knew when I loved her just like I knew when I didn't love her.

We divorced after our first son, Eric, died, and after his death, she kept our second son, Chester, a secret from me for close to five years. I was so happy Chester existed that I forgave her secret. We hurt each other a lot after Eric died.

After we divorced, Regina dated some men I hated, and an established distance was between us. But our son kept us a part of each other's lives. I was there when Chester lost teeth, had birthday parties, and graduated from schools; we raised him together. I took my son on vacations, taught him how to run, how to catch a football, how to ask a girl out for a date, how to wash a car, and how to paint a house inside and out. Regina didn't stop me from being with him, and I respected her for granting me that privilege. However, she and I stayed out of each other's private lives.

Two decades past with us existing that way; her doing her thing, and me doing mine, but I never stopped being attracted to her; the woman had always been fine as hell to me, and looking at her always turned me on sexually, and she knew it. Whenever I saw her, I found myself staring at her. I had to force myself to look away from her. It took ten years for me to be comfortable seeing her with other men despite not wanting to be with her myself.

There were times when I hated Regina. Times when if she was ablaze, I wouldn't have pissed on her to put out the fire. She has done and said some fucked-up things to me. Hate and sexual desire are two emotions that should not coincide, but they existed together where Regina and I were concerned. I would be hating her soul and still looking at her narrow hips and green eyes wanting to fuck her silly. My thing with her has always been crazy.

Standing at the sink and looking out the window into my backyard, I dialed Carol's number; she wasn't going to be happy about working on a Saturday. She answered on the second ring.

"Hey, D."

"Hey there, Carol Anne Cooper." I called her full name when I needed a favor.

"What do you want, D?" She dryly asked.

"We may have a new client."

"Ok, set the meeting for Monday unless it is an emergency."

"It might be an emergency... and the meeting is already set."

"Of course, it is. And let me guess, you want me there?"

We had both agreed that her evaluation of clients prior to the company taking them on was needed. Sometimes I took on clients that couldn't pay our fee or that required a detective agency more than a protection service; clients she complained about.

"I can handle it if you're busy." And I could have.

"How was the client referred?"

"Through Chester, the perspective client is Wilson Norton."

"The activist?"

"Yes."

She was quiet for seconds; I knew she was considering her options.

"I like what he's doing about these police shootings in the city. If he wasn't taking a stance and making people take notice, this city would sweep the shootings under a rug. Text me the address and time, and I will meet you there."

"Um, the meeting is a half hour from now."

"Of course, it is. Text me the address."

*

When I got to Norton's place, Carol was already there standing next to her little white C-Class Benz. She was parked in front of the used appliance store and standing in the orangish glow of the streetlight checking her watch. I looked down at my Benz's clock. I had two minutes before I was late. I illegally parked in front of her car; half of my car was in the yellow curb zone.

When I got out and walked to her, she looked down at the yellow paint on the curb then looked up putting her slanted eyes on me. She was dressed in a baby blue seersucker suit with a white high collar blouse and baby blue canvas oxfords. Her cornrow braids went to the back and hung passed her shoulders to the middle of her suit jacket.

"Norton is on the bell" was my reply to her unspoken objection to my parking. We walked to the small door to the south of the storefront entrance. Norton was second from the top.

"Epsilon Protection will not be paying for that parking ticket." She said without looking in my direction and pushed the doorbell. We were immediately buzzed in. I held the grey, badly in need of painting, door open for her.

Blunt smoke had the stairway cloudy. There was one apartment on the first floor. '1A' was on a gold and black decal stuck on the beat-up pine door. The golden sticker was in better shape than the door.

"Why does the smoke smell like Fruit Loops and cigars?" Carol asked.

On the second landing, a door opened, and Chester stepped into the hall. A cloud of smoke followed him.

My son looked like me in my twenties: lean and tall, he got my pudding brown skin color and my height, but he had Regina's thin black wavy hair and green eyes. Regina's hair and eyes labeled him our son.

Carol had never smoked weed, and I doubted that she had ever seen a blunt. "Flavored marijuana" was my answer to her question.

"What?" She moved toward the stairs ahead of me and began climbing up to Chester.

"The kids, smokers today, can get their weed in flavors. You are probably smelling Bubblegum Cush."

"No? Really? They have marijuana that smells like bubblegum?" she asked, looking back at me while climbing the stairs.

"Yep, and chocolate, and licorice, and strawberries, and all sorts of flavors."

When she got to the top of the stairs, Chester greeted her. "Hey, Ms. Carol. I haven't seen you since Christmas at Dad's." They hugged.

When I made it to the top, I glanced into the apartment. None of the smokers were putting out their blunts. The young activist wasn't smoking. He sat at the kitchen's raised counter on a high stool. There was an empty stool next to him. I hoped Chester was sitting there.

Two young men in blue jeans and red and gold rugby shirts were on the couch sharing a blunt, and a young lady in beige Dockers and a white polo was on a beanbag by the window with her own blunt. The girl on the beanbag had on black plastic frame eyeglasses.

When we entered the apartment, the young activist stood and walked towards us with his hand extended. I shook it.

Carol looked at the others in the room and said, "Y'all are going to have to put that shit out. We came here to talk business. I am not going to be sitting up in a dope-house."

The smokers on the couch ignored her words.

The girl on the beanbag laughed out loud and said, "This is weed, not dope, and you are here to convince us to hire you. You need to impress us." She continued to inhale the blunt smoke.

Carol didn't answer the child. She made an about-face and left through the door that Chester hadn't closed, and I followed her.

We were back outside and standing on the sidewalk next to Carol's Benz before Chester and the activist caught up with us.

"Please allow me to apologize for my associates." The activist hurried around to us and got between Carol and her car. I admired his tenacity.

"No apology required, young man." Carol had her alarm pad in her hand. She was opening the car's locks and not slowing down to hear any explanation.

"We really do need your help, Ms. Carol." Chester's words stopped her advance.

With her keys jiggling in her hands, she asked "Why?" Carol looked up at Chester and then to the young activist.

The activist answered, "Because my life is in danger, and I'm not sure where the threat is coming from. We have narrowed it down to two possible..." The kid's brown bald head snapped back, and his body was lifted inches into the air. The shots were cracking explosions. The activist's forehead was opened, and two equally large gaping holes appeared in his chest. I dove to Carol, taking her to the ground. I continued to hear shots. Chester had dropped to the sidewalk with us. The young activist was still taking rounds: to the hip, to the shoulder, to the neck, and again to the head. I pulled my pistol free and was looking into the street from beneath Carol's car. Across the street, I spotted a pair of black nylon mesh boots in a marksman stance. I stood. The shooter was still firing into the kid. My first round hit his rifle and hand, the second hit his chin, and the third and fourth went into his forehead. My rounds forced the shooter's steps backwards. He dropped to his butt and fell back onto his head. I holstered my pistol and turned to the activist. He laid on the sidewalk with the top of his head missing. Carol and Chester stood and hurried to him. I didn't. There was nothing I wanted to see.

Chester let out a wail that reminded me of his cry as a child. He collapsed to his friend.

Chapter Three

The police attention was more on me than the dead shooter. The ambulance took the dead activist away, and the media was arriving. I saw Regina with a group of reporters being held at bay. Carol and Chester were still beside me. I could tell Chester wanted to leave the scene; he was upset. No friends had ever died in his life, and the passing of his grandmother was still fresh in his heart.

Carol, Chester and I were joined by the kids from upstairs, so we were a nice little group, and despite the police trying to separate me from the group, we remained together largely due to the young girl with the thick black framed glasses.

"If you are not arresting him, we can stay with him while you are questioning him, Detective. There is no need for him to walk to your car." Her words weren't a request. She said them as a matter of fact.

Detective Dixon looked at the young girl, "What is your name, young lady?"

She didn't hesitate to answer. "Angela Gates."

Despite the noise around us, policeman with radios, ambulance sirens, reporters screaming questions and requests for admittance, Dixon had to hear the challenge in her voice; she was ready for police confrontation; she probably expected it.

Angela continued with "You need to be gathering information about the SWAT team shooter that killed our friend instead of harassing the man that ended the hateful murder's life." She had drawn the proverbial line in the sand, and she was daring cheap black suit-wearing Dixon to step across it.

I hadn't noticed that the shooter was dressed completely in police tactical gear. I saw the boots, but Angela was right, the killer was dressed in SWAT attire from his cap to his boots.

"We know how to do our jobs, Ms. Gates." Dixon turned his pitted dark brown face from Angela to me. "Price, were you here in a professional capacity?"

Detective Dixon and I had a history. His partner was one of the men Regina dated that I hated. My business involved protection, violence and murders that occurred in my life, and he and his partner were homicide detectives. We had bumped heads many times doing our jobs.

Carol's answered Dixon's question. "No, we were not, we were being sought out for possible service."

Dixon put his one crossed and the other straight eye on Carol. "It is always good to see you, Ms. Cooper."

He had tried to arrest Carol years ago for the murder of her husband. They had a history as well.

"The feeling is mutual, detective." She nodded her head but didn't smile.

"I'm going to need the weapon, Price," Dixon ordered.

I had ejected the clip, cleared the chamber, and put the pistol and clip in a plastic Ziplock before the police arrived. I handed the bag to him.

"Good boy," he said trying to agitate me. "I will do my best to get this back to you in a timely fashion."

Of course, he would do the opposite, and we both knew it. Dixon and almost every officer on the Chicago police force considered my job, the protection I offered, an intrusion on their profession, and their animosity was seldom hidden. Dixon turned away and walked toward his detective car without a goodbye.

I saw a slender Asian woman in a dark blue smock with white pants watching me from the doorway of the Korean market two stores down.

"Chester, before your friend was killed, he was about to mention two threats... do you know what they were?" I asked my son while looking at the Asian woman.

"Yes, we all know," he answered with his gaze on Dixon's back.

"Then you all should be concerned with your safety." I looked at my son. He attention was not on my words. He didn't appear to be on the street with us. He was hurting, and he wanted to leave the scene.

The young Asian woman stepped slightly out of the doorway and waved her hand. I waved back to her and beckoned her to us.

"What?" One of the two rugby shirts asked me. "Are you saying we are in danger?"

"Yes, a hell-of-a lot of danger," was my answer.

The young Asian woman stepped out of the doorway and began slowly approaching us. She was looking around at the police officers.

"Are you still trying to sell us your service?" The girl wearing the black frames, Angela, asked.

"You can't afford us," Carol answered.

My phone vibrated in my pocket. I pulled it out and saw Regina's name on the screen. I answered her call still standing with the group and watching the approaching girl. She had something in her hand.

Regina said, "They are not letting the press close, so this was your meeting. How is Chester?"

"He is shook, but he's coming around."

"I see Lee. He will get me past these uniforms," and she hung up. I saw her beelining to Detective Lee, her old boyfriend.

To Chester and his friends, I said, "This is the reality; whatever the deceased was involved in got him shot down in the middle of the street in front of witnesses, and I seriously doubt the shooter was acting on his own accord. He was probably a soldier, a sacrificial pawn. Whoever sent him is starting at the top, and they are hoping shooting Norton will derail whatever actions are planned. Norton's death is a warning… stop or die."

None of the kids said a word; they adjusted their stances and looked at each other. Then Chester said, "The calls were saying the same thing. Stop protesting or die." He spoke softly.

"What are the two threats?" Carol asked Chester.

He answered, "This girl was interning at a bank downtown, and she copied some memos, emails, and letters, and she gave them to us."

Across the street, the paramedics were loading the shooter's body into an ambulance. Dixon's partner, Lee, the dread-head, was standing next to the stretcher taking pictures of the corpse. The Asian girl walked through our crowd and came directly to me. She handed me a disc. "You might need this." I took it, and she turned away and quickly left us. We all watched her walk back into the store.

"Norton was trying to get with her." One of the rugby shirts said looking down at the disc. "They had gone out a couple of times. She probably gave you something important."

I looked down at the disc and guessed that her store camera had recorded the whole shooting.

"So, what was the bank information about?" Carol asked Chester.

"The information was about a shysty loan program." Chester hunched his shoulders. "I don't know much more, sorry."

"Where is the information?" I asked, sliding the disc into my pants pocket.

"I have it," Angela answered. "The bank is directing loan officers to steer Black and LatinX customers to a specific loan program.

The program has higher loan acceptance, but the interest rates are higher than industry standards, much higher. The memos and stuff are all from one vice-president of lending."

I asked her, "Really... is the girl still interning?"

She looked away without answering.

"I don't know, we haven't been able to reach her for two days," Chester answered. His eyes went from mine to the sidewalk. His friend's blood was sectioned off by yellow tape.

A police squad car pulled up and blasted over the speaker, "Give me that corner, clear this area. Now!"

Cops were walking up the street ordering the spectating crowd to leave. People were dispersing. Regina briskly walked up to us in yellow pants and shirt which made her light skin in look pale in the evening light. Her pen and notebook were in her hands.

"You killed the shooter?" Her question was to me.

"Hey, Ma." Chester greeted her but I had her attention. I doubted that he'd seen his mother working professionally. She didn't answer his greeting. She heard him, but when she was focused, she was focused.

"Let's continue this discussion at my office. All of us." I looked to Carol, and she nodded her head yes.

Chester looked to his group, and they too nodded their heads in the affirmative.

"Can I ride with you?" The girl in the black glasses, Angela, surprised me with the request. "Chester drives that Cadillac like it's a Porsche."

Regina stood waiting for me to confirm her information.

"Yes, I shot him," I told her.

"Ok. I will meet you all at your office." She scribbled something in her little notebook and turned from us to hurriedly walk toward Detectives Dixon and Lee.

"I don't drive my Caddy like a Porsche," my son protested to Angela.

"Yes, you do." His friends answered in unison.

I told Angela, "Sure, no problem."

*

When Angela got in my car, she didn't hesitate to join her seatbelt. "German engineering, huh?"

I had brought a Mercedes Benz S550 a year ago.

"Chester said you used to be a Cadillac man until you brought a BMW." Angela was perusing the interior of the car. "I got my eye on a 2008 328i - more than my eye, really. I gave dude three grand down this morning; they are detailing it, and they are replacing the head lights before I take delivery; they are treating me like I'm buying a new car. I'm loving it."

There were four police squad cars left on the block, and a LatinX female officer was stopping us from pulling onto the street. She was directing a news van past us.

"Customer service is important... so tell me, Angela, how do you know the intern?"

She sat upright in the seat.

"What makes you think I know her?" Her bushy eyebrows cringed together then relaxed.

The officer told Carol to pull out first; I pulled into the street following her.

"Your knowledge of the lending programs. And Chester said, 'this girl' and 'a bank.' He is uninformed. He knows the problem, but not the details. You gave details."

She looked out the passenger window for a moment or two. "Mmph," she turned back to me. "Ok yeah, she's my cousin." Angela sat back in the seat and reclined it further. "I told her not to answer any of Wilson's or Chester's calls once the threats started coming in. We don't know if it is the bank or the police threatening him, and I don't want her to get hurt."

Another officer stopped Chester's car at the corner. There was no reason to stop him. There was no traffic. The tall blond cop mouthed, "Your leader is dead" and then slid his index finger across his neck and grinned. I saw Chester raising, but both rugby shirt wearers held him in his seat. I thanked Jesus.

The cop stepped aside and waved us all on. Angela missed the whole exchange; she was still talking to me.

"I thought the bank because we have been on the police for over two years with no real threats; but one protest in front of the bank, and the real threat calls started. But Wilson and Chester thought that explanation was too simple; they believed the threats were coming from the police.

"The police protesting has gotten tense; pressure is coming from all over. Police lawyers have sent letters and called Wilson. Family lawyers of the victims have asked him to stop protesting. The mayor's minions have approached him, and even cops that did the shootings have surfaced.

"I saw one of the shooter cops leaving my plant manager's office last week. I thought I was imagining until my supervisor called me in and said I was being put back of first shift and losing my third shift differential pay, and the weak bastard said any additional media exposure could affect my journeyman training and advancement. I knew what he was saying to me was coming from above him because I sell my supervisor weed. No way he would ever say something like that to me... unless he had to."

We passed by Dixon and his partner Lee; they were standing outside a brown detective car. I had to restrain myself from flipping them the bird. I despised both of them, and my reflex was to flip them off when I saw them, but I didn't want Angela to see me acting so immature. Besides, she said something that was bouncing around in my mind, and the phrase needed clarification, so I asked her, "What do you mean, real threats?"

Again, she adjusted herself in the seat, and when I looked over at her, there was something very familiar about her face, but I couldn't put my finger on it.

She told me, "Wilson always got threats, but the threats changed. They started saying stuff like 'we going to shoot you in the head while you are eating a double cheeseburger at McDonalds on 76th and Vincennes.' We eat double cheeseburgers there almost every day. We always eat double cheeseburgers there.

"Two weeks ago, he got a call that told him if he protested in front of the bank at three pm, they would blow up his van. Our protest was set for three pm, but nobody knew it but us; we hadn't called anybody. Only our little group knew. We went through with the protest as planned, called in others, and we had a good turnout. But the creeps blew up my van while we were marching. Wilson had been driving my van for over a year."

Angela spoke as if she didn't believe what she was saying, like she doubted her own words, as if what had happened couldn't possibly be real.

"All of you are under surveillance, and it sounds like you have been for a while. Do you always meet at Norton's?"

She nodded her head in the affirmative. "Yeah, that's our spot."

Whoever was threatening them had some power. More power than the group of young activists realized.

"I'll have an associate go through Norton's place for bugs."

I looked over and saw her thinking, considering what I said. If they hadn't thought about being under surveillance, then they really were inexperienced kids, and they were in way over their heads.

"In your professional opinion, who do you think the threat is? The bank or the police?" She really didn't have a clue who they were going up against.

"Probably both, the bank and the police, and I think you are all lucky to be alive. You all have been doing good work, but it has moved to another level with Norton's death. Perhaps it is time to reevaluate your actions," I told her while turning right onto 87th Street. We drove for about three blocks without conversation.

"It's been time for me; all of this protesting was Wilson, not me. He was the real activist. Me, I was just following him. I was part of this because of him, and with him gone... you know."

She started crying, and I made a U-turn on 87th and Throop Street and pulled into our parking lot.

"Wait, I know this place; my dad's dental office is here."

Her dad? "Are you Dr. Gates' daughter?" I hadn't associated her last name with the dentist.

"Yes. You know my dad?" Again, her eyebrows cringed.

For Black people, Chicago is a big city and a small town.

"Of course, I do. We are having dinner together Sunday."

Her cringed bushy eyebrows rose above her thick black frames. "Ok. That's cool because they asked me to join them too. It sounds like we will be dining together."

Chapter Four

Due to Carol's insistence, our windowless back-storage room had been converted into a meeting room, complete with a small boardroom table, high back leather chairs, and a wall-mounted fifty-inch video monitor. The room was fly, and I was proud whenever we used it. That evening with Chester and his associates in the room, I was sitting at the head of the table, and Carol was sitting next to me typing notes on her laptop. The notes appeared on the wall-mounted white screen. The heading that appeared on the screen was "Threats," and the first one listed was *bank vice-president.*

Regina, a pit bull with a bone when it came to tracking a down a story, sat right next to Carol with her notebook open and a pen in her hand. As always, I found myself staring at Regina, and I knew she was braless by the way her breast moved beneath the yellow button-down oxford she was wearing. I forced my attention from her breast to the white board monitor.

"What is the bank vice-president's name?" a typing Carol asked the group, moving her gaze from Chester to the rugby shirt wearers, then to Angela.

The men of the group obviously had no answers. They all glanced over to Angela.

"Drayman. Theodore Drayman," she answered.

"Do you really think a banker would have someone killed?" one of the rugby shirts asked.

"Yeah," Chester answered. "I do now."

My son's realistic view of the situation spoke to his maturity and his societal awareness. I felt like he knew what was happening around him.

"But the shooter was in police tactical gear," Angela added.

"Which can be gotten from any army surplus store or on-line," Regina offered.

"I think it is a mistake to single out one threat and eliminate the other; both the police and the bank are threats. Neither should be eliminated. The plan should be for you kids to get to safety." I added my two cents.

"Ain't no kids here." Angela snapped at me pushing her black glasses up the bridge of her noses with her middle finger.

I think she was flipping me off. But she was right. Thinking of them as kids that needed protection was wrong. They were adults, but Chester was my son. I would protect him until my dying day.

"My apologies, no insult intended. You all have been doing adult work like the grown folks you are. But this danger, this direct threat, requires you to think about your safety and to leave the public eye." I was thinking about my son.

"But if we do that, what are we doing to Wilson's work, to his memory? Are we saying he's dead, so the work is over, no need to protest police shootings or crooked banks?" Chester looked at his group. "Were we only protesting because of Wilson? Are we that shallow?" He exhaled and looked down. "I truly hope not. Wilson got people involved. We got people involved. People believe that what we do changes things, and they are right."

His eyes went to the rugby shirt wearers, and they lowered their eyes.

"We got the media reporting on the number of police shootings in this city. Our protest did that." He and Angela locked eyes. "Whoever killed Wilson made a mistake. At least as far as I am concerned. His death will not be a deterrent for me. No. He will become a martyr. His death will strengthen this movement. The killers made a mistake. People are going to be more involved. I am going to be more involved." Chester's last words were targeted at me and Regina.

"Yes, I got started because of Wilson, but my commitment came from seeing the injustice. My friend got me started, my friend opened my eyes, but once I saw that what we do matters, once I saw that we can and do change things... I knew our actions were important. No way am I turning away or going into hiding. His killers made a mistake, and they are about to see what true activism is. They have stopped nothing."

I think my son was convincing himself, and the certainty in his voice made me realize that there truly were no kids in my meeting room, but my adult son was involved in a battle with foes beyond his comprehension. It was very possible that his foes had sacrificial pawns numbering in the thousands, and it was a certainty that his foes were informed.

Angela got up from her high-back chair and walked around the table to Chester. She bent down to him and wrapped her arms around him and kissed him passionately.

I saw Regina's eyes rapidly blinking. Oh, she wanted to say something to stop what she was forced to witness, but what she said was, "I am guessing the second threat is the Chicago police department. Do you have a name there as well? And why do you think the police are involved?" She was clicking her pen.

My ex-wife's hair was feathered, and the night before, I ran my fingers through it with her head in my lap. We were watching *Sanford and Son* reruns and listening to NPR on the radio. My mind drifted to memory watching her lips while she talked.

"The police want to silence us." Angela said standing from her embrace of Chester. "Mr. Price is right. The police are just as big a threat as the bank."

My son raised his head up toward Angela and said, "And they made that clear tonight."

"How?" Regina asked.

Carol typed "Police" on the screens under the banker's name and answered, "A cop laughed in our faces and made callous remarks at the crime scene tonight."

Regina was nodding her head in the affirmative, but she said, "One crude cop doesn't indicate department involvement." She faced our son.

"But Mom, the police have been on us since day one; they constantly harassed Wilson, and as of late - all of us.

I was surprised I didn't see any in the rearview mirror driving over here. The police are a threat."

I agreed with my son, but I told him, "I see Regina's point. Do you all have a name, a starting point? Has there been one officer, one administrator directly threatening you?"

He shook his head no and joined his hands together by weaving his fingers into one fist which he placed on the table. Angela walked back to her seat.

Chester said, "No, it has been the whole department. That's why we protested at police headquarters. It is the whole department. The police have shot Black people down on the westside, the southside, downtown, in Hyde Park, in Englewood, in Austin, in Pilsen; they have attacked us all over this city. They name we have... is CPD, the Chicago Police Department; they have been and continue to be a threat to us."

I heard the words coming out of his mouth. I saw him speaking, but the Chester sitting at my table speaking with such fever was not the son I saw in my mind. He was not the kid I gave a Cadillac. He was not the kid I took to see R rated movies because his mother forbade him to see them, and he was not the kid I had to bribe with hundred dollar bills to get him on the honor roll. The Chester before he was a man at war. A man committed to a fight.

One rugby shirt wearer stood, then the other stood. The first one had his phone in his hand. "Man, this was fun for the summer. It really was, but we are going back to England in three weeks. We only have two years before graduation. We can't, no, we won't risk getting shot in the head. Our mother is outside, and she is going to drive us home.

"We got involved in this because you all were involved, because Wilson was our boy, but I am not about to be a martyr for some summer fun. Call us when the funeral arrangements are being made, and we will help any way we can."

They didn't wait for objections, and none were offered. I showed them to the front door without a word. A woman was parked almost up on the sidewalk in a white Porsche Cayenne. The young men barely had the doors closed before she pulled away. I didn't blame her. If I could have, I would have drove Chester away.

When I got back to the meeting room, everyone was standing: Carol, Regina, Chester, and Angela. Regina's notebook was closed and in her shoulder bag. I wasn't sure if the meeting was fruitful for her. I looked to Carol, who looked worried. She clicked off her laptop and the wall-mounted screen went black.

"Mr. Price, I am going to ride with the speed demon, and thank you so much for your advice."

They weren't getting away that easy. "Ok, so what is the plan? If you are planning to continue with Norton's plans, then that places you in Norton's danger."

My son shook his head no. "They are not just Norton's plans; these are all of our plans; there are many more people involved than Angela and me. You were at the rally this morning; we have numbers. We built an organization."

I answered with, "An organization whose leader was just assassinated; an organization that was seeking protection for the leader due to threats, threats that proved valid. If you are going to stand in his place, then those threats are yours. Understand me?" I was telling him and Regina. She needed to know our son was in danger. What he was saying, his proposed actions, would put him at risk.

"Are you saying we need protection?" Angela asked.

"Yes, that is exactly what I am saying. If… you are going to continue with the actions that attracted Norton's killers, then yes… both of your lives are in danger. You both will be seen as the head of the organization."

The room was quiet for seconds. To me, I was stating the obvious.

"I can't stop, Dad. But there are others; someone else may get out front. I'm committed to the struggle, not necessarily the bully pulpit. My activism is not stopping with Wilson's death, but that doesn't mean I will lead the movement."

I looked to Regina, and I saw her thinking. She heard his commitment; I guessed she would try to redirect him later when his passion was lessened.

"We make up the inner circle, but we are not all there is, Mr. Price," Angela joined.

Regina cleared her throat and adjusted her shoulder bag. "In my opinion, you two are making a mistake. The threat should be identified before you proceed with any more action, any more protest. Someone killed your leader. Shot him down in the street. You should clearly identify your enemy; don't guess. And from what I have heard, I believe the investigation should start with the banker. He is the most easily identifiable threat. And how many more of you are there? How many make up your organization?"

Chester ran his fingers through his thin hair. "We have never really taken a head count, Mom. But I think we are about thirty strong, thirty people we know will show up."

I looked over at Carol, who was uncharacteristically quiet, and I quickly figured out her look of worry. She was trying to determine who would be invoiced if we protected Chester and his obvious girlfriend.

Regina continued with, "I would like to see the memos, faxes, letters, and any other correspondence that you have concerning the bank and its loan programs. If they prove authentic, media exposure is on the way."

Angela boasted, "Oh, they are real."

Regina clicked her pen without a comment.

Carol confirmed my suspicion when she asked, "How were you going to pay for Norton's protection?"

"We have funds," Chester answered.

"And can those funds be used to cover you and Angela?"

Chester considered her question, "I guess."

Carol replied, "Good."

Still running his fingers through his hair, Chester said, "But again, we may not be the ones out front; others may step up. There are a couple of people who want the podium, who want the bullhorn."

Angela added, "What he's saying is we may not be in as much danger as you all are thinking. We are two of many workers, not necessarily leaders. We were Norton's friends, but there are other activists in the group."

I told them, "Right now, the threat may believe the organization has been stalled, but once the protests start again, and someone steps up as the leader, protection should be in place."

They both appeared to be listening.

"I will keep that in mind, Dad. And after we speak to the others we will decide."

Carol quickly interjected, "I think I should make it clear that Epsilon Protection is not bidding for the business, Chester."

I almost laughed out loud. Carol did not want any part of their disorganization. Whoever stepped up as leader would have a hard time convincing Carol to provide protection services. But if my son took that position, he would be well protected.

"Oh, and Mr. Price, don't forget dinner tomorrow night," Angela said. She and Chester reached for each other and held hands. Regina looked like she wanted to spit.

"I won't."

"Cool. See you then." Angela smiled, and again she looked very familiar to me.

She and Chester walked toward the door.

"You are having dinner with that girl and Chester tomorrow?" Regina asked.

"Not just them, it turns out the Angela is Dr. Gates' daughter; and Martha invited the good doctor and his family to dinner tomorrow, and Ricky invited me."

"Mm, she doesn't strike me as a dentist's daughter. She smells like marijuana, and she seems to be lacking considerable refinement."

My ex-wife was being a mother with one male child.

"That's because she is dating your son; the girl didn't stand a chance once Chester put his arm around her," was my smiling reply.

"Did you know he was dating her?" Regina was watching them exit.

"No."

"Do you know Dr. Gates socially?" She clicked her pen and dropped it into her purse.

"No."

"His wife?"

I had to bite my lip. "Not really."

"What does that mean?"

She rolled her green marble eyes up to my eyes.

Carol was quiet and listening.

"We went to high school together; she was a couple years behind me. I really didn't know her."

I wanted to look away, but Regina kept looking straight at me.

"Mm. I will be going to the dinner with you."

She dropped her gaze.

"Perfect." And it was, the more the merrier.

Carol said, "You know these are weekend hours, and I don't work weekends, D." She had a smirk on her face. "Does their organization even have a name?" She pushed her chair up to the table

"I doubt it." To me it seemed like Norton and his friends were the nucleus of other activists. It appeared they planned actions, then got assistance. I put my arm around Regina's waist and pulled her to me. She didn't resist. "No fried fish and movies."

She rested her head against my chest. "Nope, not tonight. Who do you think shot that young man?"

She asked who shot Norton, but she was really asking... who was the threat to our son, and my answer didn't offer much information.

"The SWAT uniform the shooter wore has me twisted; it looked official, but what officer would open fire in the middle of the street in front of so many witnesses? But his dress looked like authentic SWAT." I rested my chin atop her head amidst her feathered hair.

"I think he was the police," Carol said. "And they, the police, treated his corpse with respect. They guarded it until the ambulance arrived."

Regina pulled out of our embrace and turned to Carol. "They did, didn't they. They surrounded it from the press, no pictures were taken. I bet he was an officer. Why protect a shooter like that?"

Carol walked to Regina and me. "They must be protecting one of their own."

I pulled the disc from my pocket. "Let's take a closer look. Shall we?"

*

The disc showed Norton getting shot, and our group diving to the ground, and it showed me standing and firing rounds. Further down the block another SWAT-dressed man is seen. He had a rifle as well, and he was trying to aim, but too many people were between us and him. He didn't fire. He fled out of the camera.

"Did you see him?" Carol asked me.

"I did." The shooter was not alone.

The video stopped, but it started again. This camera's focus was across the street. The shooter was seen aiming and firing his rifle repeatedly. People were seen running away from him. My bullets struck his weapon, then entered his head and chest. The video stopped again.

"Oh my God, they would have killed us all." Carol said. "I am going to assign Chester's protection tonight."

Chapter Five

The drive to Regina's townhouse was over before I could get my thoughts organized. One SWAT-attired shooter was a problem, but more than one indicated power and organization. I was able to park two townhouses down from Regina's. I pulled my .9mm from the center console and placed it inside my holster. The pistol fit snugly into the holster that was designed for the .380 that Detective Dixon had confiscated.

When I got out of my black sedan, a blue and white Chicago police cruiser slowed and put his handheld light on me. I nodded my head and kept walking. He didn't lower the light right away. I took about three steps with the light still on me. I started to stop and question the officer, but I didn't. The SWAT shooters entered my mind. The driver of the squad car lowered the light and drove off.

Maybe it was the black S550 Benz I got out of, or maybe it was the black hand-crafted Monticello straw hat I was wearing, or maybe it was my beige tailored linen walking suit, or maybe it was my black eelskin sandals, I didn't know, but whatever it was that helped the officer determine that I was not one to be harassed beyond the handheld light, made me grateful.

When I made it up Regina's tall flight of townhouse steps, she met me at the door half-naked. She still had on the yellow oxford shirt, but her bottom half was bare.

She stood blocking my entrance looking every bit the temptress.

"I saw you staring at my breast earlier, so I figured you would want to unbutton my blouse for me."

She took a step back letting me into the foyer. I backed her up against the foyer wall closing the door behind us with my foot. I jumped a bit because it slammed louder than I expected. I settled down and lightly kissed her on the lips then I slowly licked them both, then I outlined them and lightly kissed her again. I started kissing her neck; my plan was to work my way down, but I saw her nipples protruding, so I started unbuttoning her blouse. I only got three buttons open because her extending nipples demanding my suckling. My head dropped, and I sucked on her right extended nipple.

"Sweet Jesus" she moaned.

Regina enjoyed the attention I gave her breast almost as much as I enjoyed giving it. I caressed her small breast with my tongue and lips. I felt her quivering, so I kept my attention on her right breast.

"Ooooh David, damn."

I scooped my ex-wife up and carried her to the bedroom.

Our coupling was slow, lasting, and satisfying.

After, we both fell easily into a comfortable sleep, but then I heard a ringing, and it was persistent. I heard it, but I didn't want to hear. I refused the ringing's existence, and it faded away. But then I heard, "Regina Price."

I rolled away from her sitting up in the bed and hugged one of the fluffy pillows that smelled like her.

"Yes, I put in that request. What do you mean, there is nothing there? That's impossible. Ok, thank you for calling."

I rolled back over to face her and opened my eyes. She hung the phone up and remained sitting. Her attention was on the cradled phone.

"My intern was to use our database to access information concerning Theodore Drayman and Grant's Federal Bank, but she couldn't find any, and that's weird. She can retrieve information on Grant's Federal Bank from the database but not with Theodore Drayman. He is listed in the employee directory, but there is no on-line profile and no information other than his name and title. He has no presence in the database or on Google. Who can ghost like that? What bank VP doesn't have an internet footprint?" She stood from the bed and walked out of the bedroom. I knew she was going to her office computer.

The white numbers and letters of her clock read 4:45am. It was Sunday morning, and I had no plans of getting out of the bed. I hugged the pillow tighter and felt myself drifting off, but then my phone rang. I knew where it was; it was next to her nightstand clock with my keys and my pistol, but I kept my eyes closed. Maybe it was a wrong number. It rang two more times before I answered without looking to see who was calling.

"Mr. Price? David Price?"

"Yes."

"My name is Langston Waters. I was one of Wilson Norton's guardians."

"Ok."

"I do apologize for calling at this hour, but my cousin, Detective Johnathan Lee, gave me your number. He told me you shot and killed the man that murdered my ward."

He got my attention. I opened my eyes, sat up, and braced my back against Regina's headboard.

"Ok?"

"Johnathan is concerned because the man who shot Wilson was a police officer, and he has reason to believe that there were others there to assist, and he believes your being there was unexpected, and their plans changed because of you. He gave me a name."

His words were confirmation of what we suspected, but what I hoped wasn't true. Norton was killed by a Chicago police officer, and the information was coming through Detective Lee who has never been of assistance to me.

"Detective Johnathon Lee gave you this information?" The police detective was one of the men I hated that Regina dated.

"Yes, and he said you might be doubtful; he also instructed me to inform you that the officer should be contacted soon."

"What's the name?"

"A patrolman, Thomas Pinker."

"The white cop that shot the seventeen-year-old Black student?"

"That's the one."

"Shit."

"Johnny said he walks to church every Sunday, a four-block walk. He thinks you should approach him on his walk home after church. He says you should ask him why he – a suspended police officer - was at the scene last night dressed in tactical gear. Johnny said be direct when you ask. The church service is from 10:15 to 11:45."

It sounded like Detective Lee knew more than he told his cousin. And what made the detective think I would follow his directives? Something was going on.

"Pinker was there last night, at Norton's?"

"That's what Johnny said. The church is located at 3112 South Green Street. I'm texting you the patrolman's picture that Johnny sent me. Should I meet you at the church?"

"I'm sorry?"

"Where should I meet you?"

"You are a social worker, right? This may be a little out of your comfort zone."

There was no way an amateur sleuth was tagging along.

"It won't be. I was military police in the Marine Corps."

I was impressed, a Black MP in the US Marines, but I didn't know him.

"Why do you want to come?"

"Wilson was like a son to me, Mr. Price. I called Johnny to get your name as part of my own investigation. I was curious as why you weren't arrested, and Johnny explained what you do." He paused then stated, "You didn't do your job, did you?"

The motherfucker had some balls.

"Look, Mr. Waters, Wilson Norton was not under my protection when he was killed. I was there because my son wanted to discuss protection services for Mr. Norton. I can't help you with this."

He had pissed me off, and I was hanging up the phone when I heard, "You are a gun for hire, right? I want to hire you. I'm going to find out who is responsible for Wilson's death."

Without hesitation I told him, "You know who is responsible. He was killed by a police officer."

"No, police officers, not just one. Johnny says there were more on the scene."

I was still going to hang up.

"That is not how I work, Mr. Waters. You should leave things to the police. If Lee knows all of this, he will get an investigation started."

"Johnny said you are a bodyguard slash private dick. My plan is to investigate my ward's killing further, and I think I will be threatened by the police that killed him. I need you to protect me while I find out who killed him. Now… is that how you work?"

I did want the case, but I didn't want to be bothered with Waters.

"Mr. Price, if the police killed Wilson, even with Johnny being part of the department there will be complications and cover ups. I know how the police work, how they defend each other. The fact that one of them was bold enough to shoot Wilson down in the middle of the street speaks to their delusional privilege. Finding justice will be left to me, and I need help. Your professional assistance will be appreciated, and I will pay for your service."

A paying client was a thing of beauty, so I said, "Ok. Meet me a block north of the church at ten. I will be in a black Benz. Plan on going to the church service."

Waters confirmed with "I will see you then."

We disconnected just as Regina flipped on the bedroom lights.

She stood naked looking down at me sitting against her headboard. What she said out of her mouth, shook me again.

"David, I want you to sell your home in Englewood. My place here is nearly sold. I have picked out five three-bedroom condominiums for us to look at; they are located from the south loop to the gold coast. My agent feels confident that she could sell your home for a profit. The five locations that I found are all accepting of pets, and..." She stepped away from the light switch and stood with her slender thighs against the bed. "I want us to get married again. A small ceremony at Ricky's and Martha's home should suffice. What do you think?"

Her face was tender, and her eyes were hopeful. She really didn't know how I would answer. My jones got hard.

I stood up from the bed and put my naked body against her and said, "Yes, yes and yes."

I thought that was a cool way to answer, but inside my head I was jumping for joy. Hell yes, I would marry her fine ass again.

She was up on her tippy toes kissing me, then she pushed me on the bed. I was laying on my back with my jones pointing to the ceiling. She got on me and mounted me with her knees up. My thought was to flip her over and go at missionary, but she wasn't having it. If I tried to move, she would press down with all her weight. She wanted to stay on top and keep riding me, and that was what she did.

*

Like me, Waters had on a brown suit with no tie. His white dress shirt was opened at the collar, and his dark brown shoes were polished to a gleam. He had parked his bronze Volvo sedan on the opposite side of the street, about four car lengths ahead of me. I got out my car as he was approaching. It was a sunny morning, and he stopped in the middle of the street and waited for me to get to him.

"Mr. Price?"

"Yep, Mr. Waters?"

He looked to be in his mid-thirties, and he was built like a runner. Waters stood about 5'8" without an ounce of noticeable fat on his face. He gave me a firm handshake with no smile. His hair was cut in a close fade with waves going to the back. His brown skin had an orange tint to it like a tiger.

"It's probably a white church," he said.

It was a sunny morning, and we walked towards the tiny church watching only white people entering.

"That would be my guess," I said, agreeing. "My plan is to sit at the back avoiding too much attention."

Walking alongside of him, I saw the butt of a pistol under his suitcoat in a shoulder holster.

"I hope you a have a permit for that firearm?"

"I do."

We stepped up the eight concrete stairs through the dark maple doors with brass hinges and entered the church. The church was too small for us to go unnoticed. As soon as we entered the sanctuary, the congregation saw us. I progressed up one row from the last and made it to the center of the pew bench and sat. Waters followed me. Members walked by and sat in pews ahead of ours. Some heads turned and looked over their shoulders at us.

The sun shone through the stained-glass windows illuminating pink fat faced cherubs, white doves, golden angels, and faces of a white Jesus with his blue eyes looking toward the heavens. We, Waters and I, were the only visible faces of color within the church. An usher closed the sanctuary doors, and the service started with the choir singing a hymn. I spotted Pinker in the third row. He hadn't looked back at us.

The service was boring. I was not moved to clap, say amen, pat my foot, or sing along. When it ended, I was grateful and ready to leave. We stood and left as soon as the sanctuary doors were opened. We were not approached about church membership or invited to Bible study, and the minister looked a bit perplexed about seeing us in the greeting line. I shook his hand despite his confusion and progressed down the stairs. We moved to the left of the stairs which gave us a side view of the church, and that proved to be a good move because Pinker was hurriedly exiting through a side door.

We didn't have to run; rapid steps caught us up with him.

"Mr. Pinker, do you have minute?" I asked.

It was only he and us walking down the residential block he chose.

"I have already talked to the press. I have nothing more to say."

He didn't slow down or turn around.

"We are not here about your trial." Waters said.

Pinker stopped and turned around. He looked us up and down and actually sneered. "Then what? What do you two African Americans want to talk to me about?"

I had never heard the term African American sound so much like nigger in my life. The spoken words were encased in his hate. He clearly said African Americans, but I clearly heard niggers.

He was shorter and thinner than Waters. Me being 6'2" put me over both of them, and way over Pinker.

When I quickly stepped to him, his hand went to his hip for his pistol, but he wasn't in uniform, so he had no pistol.

I informed that "It's not the shooting you are on trial for that I want to talk to you about, and I am not with the press. I'm here to talk to you about last night's shooting."

The lids covering his gray eyes started blinking rapidly. "Last night's shooting? What the hell are you talking about? I wasn't involved in a shooting last night." He tried to step back from me, but the yard hedges of the brick bungalow home stopped his retreat.

Waters told him, "Tribune photos say different; they show you in SWAT attire at the scene."

I liked how Waters was applying pressure with the lie. There were no photos, but it may have been Pinker on the video clip. He was considering running, but Waters was to his left, and I was directly in front of him and to his right.

"I was home. My mother will testify to that."

I almost laughed in his face for depending on his mother for an alibi.

"You are also on the liquor store footage." Waters added a statement that might have been true.

Pinker released a long breath and his shoulders went down. "What do you want?" He looked at Waters, not at me, despite me being the closest to him.

"Why were you, a suspended Chicago police officer, at the scene last night?" Waters continued.

Other neighborhood church members had made it to the block, and there were a couple of cars driving down the residential block as well. Looking around and seeing the others on the block, Pinker began to regain a little spine.

"You are not the police, and you are not the press. So, chances of me answering your questions are slim to none."

Experience had taught me that sometimes people didn't answer initial questions. But later, when other pressures were applied, they got talkative. I was thinking we were at that point with Pinker, and I was pulling a card from my wallet when Waters pulled his pistol from the shoulder holster and struck Pinker across his face, twice.

I was startled, but Pinker was shocked to attention and scared as hell. All of his bravado fled.

Waters told him to "think about this, whoever we are, we got enough pull to see Tribune photos and liquor store footage of you and the other stupid cops. At least two other cops, right?"

He shoved the barrel of his .357 into Pinker's left eye socket. "I got enough pull to blow your redneck brains out on this sidewalk and keep walking like nothing happened. Now, motherfucker, who was with you?"

Apparently, Pinker believed Waters because he spilled the beans: "Alfred Harris, Jeffery Lanham, and Peter Redding." I recognized the officers' names; each was involved in questionable police shootings that got media attention.

Alfred Harris was a SWAT officer who claimed a handcuffed Black female mental patient reached for his holstered gun, resulting in her being shot three times in the head. Jeffery Lanham was a fat gout-ridden police sergeant who shot a fleeing preacher's son in the back and head and expressed no remorse when only a Bible was discovered in the boy's hand. Peter Redding was caught on videotape shooting a Black man who was on his knees with his hands in the air. Redding was seen pulling his pistol's trigger even after the clip emptied; the city's citizens saw Redding throw his empty pistol at the man's bullet-riddled head when the bloodied corpse was on the ground.

Neither Pinker nor Waters appeared to be breathing. Seconds passed with the .357 in Pinker's eye. Waters pulled the hammer back on his revolver. Pinker's gray eyes bucked, and his knees gave way. He dropped to the lawn face first. He landed on the side of his face with his eyes twitching. People that were walking down the block stopped and looked at us. We were drawing a lot of attention; two Black men standing over a white man lying in the grass. Waters and I quickly walked away.

Chapter Six

I was hungry, so I had Waters meet me at Norman's Bistro. He obviously was not the typical social worker, or maybe he was. I didn't have any social worker buddies, so I really didn't know how they reacted to situations, but I wasn't expecting him to pistol whip a police officer on the street in broad daylight. Perhaps being ex-military police allotted him some psychological privilege, but whatever the reason, I enjoyed his unpredictable reaction.

Wilson Norton's killer still hadn't been identified to the media, and people, mostly Black people, were asking why not. They were asking through the television, through radio talk shows, and through internet podcast. People in the city wanted to know who shot Wilson. I was thinking the shooter had to be one of the names Pinker gave us, and if he would not have fallen out in the grass, I would have confirmed it. But Detective Lee knew Wilson's killer, and he knew the killer was a cop.

Waters had shed his suit coat and holster. He entered the cozy restaurant in a white dress shirt and brown suit pants. I stood and waved him over to my table by the window. For the past three months, Regina and I had reserved the window table for Sunday brunch; that Sunday, we were both working, but the reservation was standing, so I invited Waters to a meal.

He sat talking. "I just heard one of the names that Pinker gave us on the news." He nodded his head towards the television that was playing over the piano. It was replaying footage of last night's shooting, but I couldn't hear the broadcast. "The man who murdered Wilson was Peter Redding. They reported his name, but not the fact that he was a Chicago police officer."

I had shot and killed a Chicago police officer. Regina and Carol both guessed it, but Waters, Lee, and Pinker confirmed it. Thinking I might have killed a cop was a lot different from knowing I killed a cop. A new, a more alert awareness was required in my life.

I killed a solider of Chicago's largest military force. Unknowing, I left the house with only one pistol and no extra clips; I should have had three pistols and at least two extra clips for each. My situation had changed.

It wasn't surprising that the city didn't release Redding's police officer status, but city and police officials wouldn't be able to keep his occupation a secret for long.

"How did you know Pinker was with other police officers?" I asked Waters.

"That's what Johnny said. He said Pinker was there with others, and cops do things in groups. I did a quick Google search of each name Pinker gave us, and those cops are in the same situation as Pinker; they were all involved in shootings. Wilson and his followers were bringing media attention to police shooting incidents. Cases that had historically been swept under the rug were being kept in the public eye; those cops wanted to stop Wilson."

Waters was ex-military police. I guessed he was speaking from firsthand knowledge. I remembered each incident, and Waters was right, the shootings were fading from public consciousness. Wilson's protest was keeping the incidents in the media, reminding people of the injustice. Yes, those cops wanted him dead, and the protests stopped.

"You're right, every name Pinker gave was involved in a police shooting." I had killed one of their group. I was swimming a pool of piranhas and bleeding out the ass, and Detective Lee knew the situation.

Waters said, "Cops are joiners; they have a wolf pack mentality, and since Wilson and his group were and are threats, it makes sense that the shooters would group together to attack a common enemy."

The waitress brought Waters a menu. I'd already ordered: salmon coquettes, red beans and rice, and broccoli with cheese sauce. He picked the steam table over the menu, so the waitress brought him a plate, and he went to select his meal. Sitting alone at the table, my mind went over the police threat.

I was hoping that Redding was part of a rogue group because there was no fighting the entire Chicago Police Department, but I could expose a rogue group. Lee turned Pinker over to us. That meant he wanted him exposed, and I was hoping he was not the only cop who wanted the bad cops removed; the group, the shooter cops, had to be uncovered for the rogues that they were, and Lee had dropped that burden in my lap. I knew the motherfucker wasn't doing me a favor.

The information Lee got to me through Waters pulled me deeper into the murk of piranhas. He couldn't expose his brothers in blue, but I could. He was using me. To survive the situation, I had to turn the Chicago police force against a group of their own - that was my only solution, and I needed help. I needed to use the same tool Wilson used, the media. Regina could help in that area.

Looking out the restaurant window at the small tables used for outside dining, I thought about my ex-wife, and then I thought her marriage proposal, and my tense mind relaxed a bit. She wanted a small wedding, and I was cool with that, but I wanted both my brothers and my parents there. Ricky Brown would be my best man.

Selling the house in Englewood, she probably expected a major protest from me, and at thirty-six or forty-six years of age, I would have offered her one, but at fifty-six, my community work had slowed, and I have learned how to help without being shoulder-to-shoulder in the battle, and besides, a brother was ready for some luxury residential living. Regina said she'd picked five luxury condos for us to review.

I was so deep in thought about Regina and getting married that the detectives' approach went unnoticed until they sat at the table with me.

"What the hell, Price, why do you eat at this high ass place, six-dollar coffee and shit?" It was cheap suit wearing Detective Dixon. He sat to my right and Detective Lee sat to my left. God, they looked like cops.

German Shepherd expressions shaped their faces as they looked around the room.

If I'd not known how good the food was going to be, my appetite would have been spoiled. Those officers of the law topped my least favorite people list.

"Detectives, what a pleasant surprise."

Lee shook his head no, causing his red locs to dangle. "Nope, Price, we are not going down that path." He scooted his chair up to the table. "We don't have to be civil – we don't like you, and you don't like us. No small talk needed. We getting to it and leaving." And to Dixon he said, "We are not staying to eat, so don't worry about the prices." Back to me he said, "So Pinker rolled over, that was good, and Redding has been identified as the killer. The two other pricks, Harris and Lanham, have to be spooked. Two cops in their little secret group are out in the open."

Waters must have updated Lee with the other cops' names, which was cool. Waters returned from the steam table with his plate in hand and sat. He jumped right into the conversation. "I don't think they will be spooked, not really. They are filled with white cop privilege. If they think Wilson's people are still stirring up the media, they will continue to act against the group without fear. Now, Pinker telling them he got visitors might cause them to reassess the situation, but they are still very much a threat to Wilson's organization."

Which meant they were a threat to my son. I agreed with Waters; the shooter cops were a threat.

"Redding is dead, but I want the other three fired and exposed. We got the names for you, so what are you going to do?" Waters asked Lee.

Cross-eyed Dixon was looking down at Water's plate that was filled with fried cabbage with carrots and green peppers, pork chops smothered with brown gravy, and glistening sweet potatoes.

"What do you mean?" Lee asked Waters.

I answered him with, "You got four shooter cops at a scene where an activist who was fighting against police shootings is murdered. I think you as a police officer should be doing something."

Lee reared back in the restaurant chair, huffed and sort of laughed. "I did something, I got Pinker's name to you. Now, you got two other names to help you do whatever." He looked down at Waters' plate too. "That food does look good."

Dixon was waving the waitress over. She came to the table with two menus and each detective took one. A server brought me my plate and each cop looked hungrily at it.

"Brunch is the menu or the steam table?" Dixon asked the waitress.

"Yes," she answered waiting.

I spoke as the waitress stood there, not waiting for Lee to give her an order. "Are you saying you will not investigate the officers, the names we gave you?"

The waitress left our table.

Without looking up from the menu, Lee said, "I have nothing to investigate. I gave you Pinker's name. The shooter, Redding, is dead. What the else is there?" He looked up at me and then Waters and then back at me. "Yo ass killed a cop, justified shooting or not, everybody ain't gonna be pleased about that."

His stare was saying a lot.

"There is a threat to Wilson's organization," Waters stated.

"We don't investigate threats; we are homicide detectives," Dixon chimed in, talking to Waters.

"If I was in your situation, Price, I would be about the business of exposing the other two cops," Lee told me while reading the menu.

"Yep," Dixon said also reading the menu, "because policeman don't like cop killers, and your security guard ass is a cop killer."

*

Waters and I were sitting in the front seats of my car.

"I expected more from Johnny."

"Like what?" I asked.

"Anger, being upset about cops shooting people, something more than them smacking over brunch. He acted like him giving me Pinker's name was a big deal."

I rolled down the window with the air conditioner on and spat on the curb. I was aiming for the black grated sewer cover but missed. "It was a big deal. He opened one of his own to investigation. Because of him, we know who the threat is, and why they are a threat. The shooters must be acting rogue, and they are probably an embarrassment to decent cops.

"People loved Wilson Norton, and his death will have ramifications that neither the city nor the police department want. When people find out that it was a cop that killed Wilson, the shit is going to hit the fan." I was certain of that.

"And when they find out that Redding was part of a group of shooter cops..." Waters trailed off.

"Exactly. Lee is using us to do what he can't do, cut out some bad cops."

And I was hoping that the exposing, the cutting out, was more than Lee's goal; hopefully, other cops were aware of the group and wanted them gone as well.

"That could be dangerous."

"Ain't no could be about it; getting involved in this shit is dangerous as fuck."

I kept the window down and looked at him hard. "Wilson's killer is dead. What will getting involved in all this do for you?" I had to expose the officers for my protection and the protection of my son; that was not the case for Waters.

He leaned back in the seat, and he inhaled and exhaled deeply. He gave the question moments of consideration.

"It's just wrong. What those policemen are doing is wrong."

I told him, "So is getting killed, which is a reality if you get mixed up in all of this. We are talking about dirty cops, and there is always more to it than what is seen on the surface; we see four dirty cops, but those four are connected to a whole force."

My phone rang and the screen read 'asshole.' It was Detective Lee. I answered.

He quickly asked, "How did y'all leave Pinker?"

"In the grass. He fainted."

"He didn't faint; the fucker had a massive heart attack. He's dead; and somebody snapped pictures of you two walking away from him and of my cousin his holstering his .357. I'm looking at y'all now on the television. If the other two officers didn't know about you, they know about you now. Good fuckin' luck."

And he hung up.

"What?" Waters asked.

"We made the news."

I dialed Carol's number. She answered with "I'm watching you on television right now."

I told her, "Meet me at the office in a half hour and call Marcus."

"See you there." Carol ended the call.

I looked to Waters and said, "Someone took pictures of us with Pinker. He didn't faint; he had a massive heart attack. He's dead, and they took a picture of you holstering your weapon. The shooters will find out who we are soon enough. Now you do need my protection."

He sat up in the seat and said, "Ok. I guess the danger just got real."

He had no idea. I asked him, "How far do you live from here?"

"Six or seven blocks." We needed to get rid of his car.

"Ok. I will follow you home. Are you married?"

"Yes, with four kids."

He was risking his personal safety with a family. "Damn, what was you thinking?" I didn't mean to say that out loud.

He looked at me then his gaze went straight ahead, out of the front windshield.

"I don't know. I reacted. I wasn't thinking. I have been in react mode since I found out Wilson was shot and killed. My wife begged me to calm down. She begged me not call you, and she begged me not to go to that church."

Life has taught me wives should be listened to. I didn't tell Waters that because life was teaching it to him.

"Ok, we will call your family from my office. Follow me. I have a safe place for your car." Taking his car to his family home might have endangered his whole family. Hiding his car was part of hiding him. Police searched for vehicles first. Hiding his would buy us some time.

*

We drove to Buddy's hand carwash on 89th and Ashland. I called ahead and told Buddy I needed to rent a secure parking space for at least two days. He agreed. When Waters drove into the carwash, Buddy greeted him like a friend. Again, the social worker surprised me. They exchanged dap and Buddy told me, "No fee, D."

I have rented spaces from Buddy for fifteen plus years, and no discount has ever occurred despite my many negotiating attempts. Buddy is known for squeezing a dollar tight enough to make George Washington walk off the bill.

The streets say he charges his own mother interest on the money he gives her between Social Security checks, and I know homeless people that refuse to work at the carwash because of the paltry pay Buddy offers. So, him not charging me to store Waters' car was way out of character.

I didn't get out of my car, but I rolled the window down to clearly hear what Buddy was saying to me. His name used to be called Buck Teeth Buddy, but he lost his front buck teeth in a fist fight with Ricky Brown eighteen years ago, which might be another reason why a discount has never been extended.

Grinning and showing the space in his teeth, Buddy said, "Waters helped get my son into college with a scholarship. Whatever he needs, he got it from me."

Buddy's son was nowhere close to college material. Buddy wouldn't let his son wash a car alone, work the register, or talk directly to customers. At the carwash, Buddy Jr's job was to dry the towels, not wash the towels, but to dry the towels and pass them out to the car washers. I could think of no college that would admit him for any program.

I watched as Waters slipped back into his holster and suit coat and got into my car. Buddy bid us farewell, and I made the three-point turn maneuver within the carwash and pulled back onto the avenue.

"How did you get Buddy's son into a school?"

I had forgotten to tell Carol to draw up a contract for Waters, but that wouldn't be a problem for her.

Waters was clicking his seat belt closed. "You're kidding, right? Buddy Jr. was an all-state wrestler in his freshman and sophomore years. The only reason he didn't wrestle varsity was coaches in the city were afraid of him because they didn't know how to stop him from wrestling once a match ended.

"Something would click inside of him once he started wrestling; he broke a kid's hip, a couple of kids' arms, and he sprang a neck or two. But this coach in Florida, his wife is a therapist; she flew up half a dozen times to counsel with Buddy Jr., and she convinced her husband that he was ready to wrestle. The coach got him a full ride."

The sun was still bright, and the pretty day remained, refusing not to be noticed. Despite developing into a police target, I saw the beautiful day and smiled at it.

"How did a coach in Florida know about Buddy Jr.?"

"I sent him some match tapes down to him and told him the whole story. He told his wife, and she got involved. Buddy's Sr's thanks should go to her."

I was determined to keep Waters safe. The community couldn't afford to lose him.

"How old are your kids?" I asked him.

"The oldest is ten going on twenty-one. She is smart as a whip and keeping her engaged is giving us a run for our money. When she is idle, she gets in trouble, and not a little bit of trouble either: spying on the neighbors with a telescope trouble. She made a telescope out of tin cans, mirror pieces, and her mother's old eyeglasses. And get this, Price, she removed her baby sister's wart with sewing thread, a cube of ice, and alcohol. The ER doctor said he couldn't have done a better job. She is truly her mother's child, smart as hell. What about you, any children?"

He started smiling when he was talking about his family, and he got relaxed, which was a good thing because tense clients make the job harder.

"I have a son, Chester. He is an adult. He and Wilson were friends which is how I got involved."

Wates nodded his head. "I know him. Chester Price, he graduated from Howard with Wilson, a very nice young man. I don't know why I didn't make the name connection."

He exhaled again and looked out the passenger window. I think the gravity of the situation was settling on him. He was in over his head; there was no denying that.

When I pulled into my parking lot, I told him, "Epsilon Security is the best protection service in this country. You are in good hands, Mr. Waters, believe me. Let's go inside."

Chapter Seven

As a Black man in America, my relationship with the police has been complicated, and what made it complicated was my home training. I was raised to see every human as a person; I was raised to see the man inside the doctor's lab coat as a person, not just a physician. My daddy was fond of saying, "Every man puts his pants on the same, one leg at a time. The preacher, the teacher, and the judge got to eat and pee just like you." I was raised to see the person within the profession.

The woman standing behind the cash register was a lady that could have been my auntie; she was not a machine taking my order. She was a person; that is what I raised to believe. And, for most of my life, I have tried to see the person behind the position, but there have been several police officers who blinded me to their personage, and they forced me to see only the uniform.

I was nine years old pitching pennies at the park, and a police squad car rolled up on us, and the Black officer said, "you little niggas out here gamblin'." The Black officers got out of the squad car and told us to place our hands on the curb with our fingers extended which we did, not knowing what to expect. The officers began stomping on our hands smashing our fingers into the concrete curbs. With my fingers bleeding, I could not see past the uniform to man; all I saw was the uniform.

My first arrest happened at thirteen with a group of five other boys; we were brought in for curfew violation. Since it was my first time being arrested, I was scared. The six of us, all pre-teens, were in one cell. Three policemen came into the holding cell, and the officers took their uniform belts off and beat us to tears.

"If yo' mamas won't teach you to respect the law, God-damn-it we will," one of them screamed while slinging his belt.

Again, I didn't see people; I saw uniforms.

As child, I learned to fear the police because what was fun in my mind was obviously wrong to them. Perhaps they were trying to direct us away from criminal activity, but all I saw was grown cops beating on kids, and I learned police officers were to be avoided.

A week or so after my curfew arrest and beating, an Officer Friendly came to our classroom to establish community relations with children. He told us the police department's mission was to serve and protect the community. He instructed us to see police squad cars as vehicles of friendship, and if we were ever in trouble, we should go to them for help. I listened to him, but while he was talking all I could think about was the beating we received in holding and police uniform belts lashing across our backs and buttocks. There was nothing friendly about the beating, and I decided that the police were liars.

*

Carol was not happy; it was Sunday afternoon; the end of her weekend, and she was working. By the time

Waters and I got to the office, she had called in Marcus and put together some information on Pinker and Redding. I walked to my desk and saw photos of both men and the report. I directed Waters to her desk by pointing to it.

"Carol, this is Mr. Waters, our new client."

She stood in her pink two-piece business suit with white silk blouse and extended her hand. A six foot, five inches, two-hundred-forty-pound, cherrywood brown Marcus was sitting to side of Carol's desk; he also stood and shook Waters' hand. Marcus was wearing the black Adidas running suit that I gave him for Christmas. All of us sat after the introductions.

At my desk, I was glancing over the reports; Carol had done a good job. There were several articles written on Pinker's and Redding's shooting incidents. I would read the report in detail later. It was time to bring everyone up to speed.

I addressed them all. "All right, this is the situation. Mr. Waters has become the target of some Chicago police officers. It is speculated that the officers were attempting to assassinate Wilson Norton and the principals of his organization. One of the officers did assassinate Wilson. The man who opened fire on us last night, Carol, was a Chicago police officer, and he was there with three other officers." I said Carol's name, but I looked at everyone in the office.

"Us being there, me and you, Carol, caused Wilson to leave the apartment, and that forced the shooters to change their assassination plans. The street shooting was not supposed to happen. I'm sure their plan was to kill them all in the apartment."

That had to be their plan. They were going to storm the apartment and shoot everyone in the room.

"Why?" Carol asked. "Why did the police want to kill them?"

The answer was simple. "Wilson and his group are bringing too much attention to the police shootings that have happened this year. They are disturbing the standard police cover-ups. The system that would normally protect these officers is being challenged by Wilson's protest; he and his group are attracting too much media attention, and people in the city and across the country are responding. Wilson Norton became a threat to the status quo, and to business as usual in this city."

Carol didn't raise her hand, she sort of waved at me with her extended index finger. "And Mr. Waters?"

I pushed back a bit from my desk and rocked back in the chair, "Mr. Waters was seen in the presence of one of the officers that was targeting Wilson. The officer had a fatal heart attack while in the company of Mr. Waters and myself, pictures were taken, and I am certain the other officers are in the process of identifying us both."

Carol continued with, "Ok, it was both of you on the television, and for clarity, are you saying we are protecting Mr. Waters from the Chicago Police Department?" Her eyes were directly on me.

I scooted back up to my desk. "Yes, the people we are protecting Mr. Waters from are Chicago police officers, shooter cops that have shot and killed Black people."

Waters fidgeted in his chair in response to my words. "Shooter cops. Damn, Mr. Price. Did you have to say it like that? You make them sound like a hit squad."

I told him, "They are a hit squad."

I let my words sink in. He needed to be aware of the threat.

Moments passed before I said, "Marcus, I need you to do that computer thing you do with the phone, so Mr. Waters can call home without people knowing where he is calling from."

Marcus nodded his brown basketball head in the affirmative. "No problem, Mr. Price. Which phone?"

Carol handed him her mobile and pushed her laptop to him. She stood and came over to my desk and sat in the side chair.

"Safe house?"

Five years ago, we purchased a house to help addicts who were released from treatment with nowhere to stay. The home provided temporary housing for up to ninety days. My recovering brother and his recovering wife ran the home, but I kept the basement apartment for Epsilon Security clients needing protection.

"Yep, at least for two days."

With Carol's phone in hand, Waters asked, "Is there a private area?"

"Marcus, show Mr. Waters to conference room," I directed, and they both stood and walked to the back.

"Ok, so you want me to assign Marcus first?"

"Yep, follow him with Keith, then Aaron. After that, the situation should have changed. Replace Lamar with Sean and Patrick on my son."

Her thin eyebrows went up. "That's only two days of coverage. You think this will all wrap up in two days?"

"If I do my job right," was my answer. I started re-reading the report she had compiled. "Good work on this."

She glanced down at the report. "Yeah, I figured you would want it. Looks like they worked out of the same precinct twice before."

I turned a page. "I see that. Neither has advanced much career-wise."

Reading along with me she said, "One lived with his mother, and the other was divorced three times and is currently living alone."

The report clearly placed Pinker in my mind. "Officer Pinker is the one who shot that student for sneaking on the back of the bus. Snatched him off the bus and shot him for not having bus fare. That was a damn shame." Remembering the incident brought up the same anger that was present when I first heard of the shooting.

Carol leaned back in the side chair and unbuttoned her pink jacket. "The protest around that shooting was my introduction to Wilson Norton. I had seen him on the news, but I didn't learn his name until the student shooting."

The same was true for me. "Chester told me his name, but I knew of his work as well. I marched when they were protesting the kid who was on his knees with his hands up when they shot him."

Carol looked up from the report. "Yes, that was Officer Redding's doing."

Damn, two dead officers. Two dead officers that had shot and killed two young Black men, and both officers were dead within a 24-hour period, and I was present at both deaths.

"Why are you smiling?" Carol asked.

It felt like I was grinning, not smiling. "Nothing" was my answer. But I continued with, "I can't help but think those shootings would have never been brought to public attention if not for Norton. And the truly sad part is that we all know there have been others. Other shootings that were not protested against."

I was still reading the report when she asked, "And you are thinking the cops that did these shootings, the ones Norton were protesting, that those cops were out there to gun down Norton and his group last night, but we showed up and interrupted their plans?"

I closed the report. "Yep, that is exactly what I'm thinking. And Detective Lee planted the seed. It was him that sent Waters to me with Pinker's name. He is responsible for getting me into this mess."

Carol leaned back in the chair and shook her head no. "To be honest, D., Chester called us in."

I ignored her words because it felt better being angry at Detective Lee. "And now, thanks to Pinker having a heart attack and dying, and someone taking our pictures at the scene, the shooter cops know we are involved, but... I have a slight advantage. Pinker gave me their names."

"And how will that help you?"

"Because I get to strike first."

"What do you mean – strike first?"

I didn't answer her because Waters and Marcus stepped back into the office.

"How was your family?" I asked Waters while feeling Carol's eyes burning into the side of my face.

"My wife is upset. She saw the pictures on the news, and there are photos of me striking Pinker with my pistol. I am wanted for questioning. She believes I should turn myself in."

He was sounding like he agreed with her, so I told him, "Later we will deal with the police after the confusion settles. There is no way I am putting you in police custody after Pinker's heart attack."

Waters looked from me to Carol, then back to me.

"My wife thinks if I explain everything to the police things will work out, and I was thinking Johnny could keep me safe. He is a police detective." His tone became defensive as if I was stopping him from doing what he wanted to do.

I closed the report and pushed my chair slightly away from the desk and plainly told him, "You and your wife are both wrong. Lee already helped you; he warned you about the police looking for you, and the police department he works for is larger than him.

"Understand this, these men shot down Wilson in the middle of the street. They have no fear; they are protected by the legal system and this city. You are a David against a Goliath. The safest thing you can do right now is hide. Which is what you are going to do." I was not giving him a choice because he was talking foolishness. He was making a life decision based on his wife's fear.

Waters handed Carol her phone back.

"I disagree, Mr. Price. I gave my wife this address. She is en route to pick me up, and then we are going to the police. I should have listened to her earlier."

He and his wife were inexperienced in dealing with powerful threats. They didn't know how powerful the adversary that was organizing against us was. I was certain the police had already accessed his home phone line. I didn't think it was time for Waters to start listening to his wife, so I told him, "That would be a serious mistake."

"I don't think so," and the finality in his tone stopped my objections.

My head lowered, and my fingers ran across my bald head. I looked up at him with as much warning in my expression as possible.

"Be careful, my brother. At least call Lee before you go into a police station. Have him take you in."

He'd given his wife my address, so the police were on their way to my office. We all needed to leave. Waters sped up the inevitable danger.

"I will; that is good advice. Do I owe you for your services today?"

Before Carol could answer, I told him, "Yes, you will receive an invoice, and don't forget about your car at Buddy's, and I am going to have Marcus stay with you until the end of the day. You won't even know he's with you unless you need him."

I saw him thinking of arguing, but he didn't.

"Thank you, Mr. Price."

My phone rang and Regina's name was on the screen. I answered.

"Hey D., saw you on the news."

"Was it my good side?" I stood from my desk gathering the report.

"Yeah, it was. Are you going to the police?"

"Nope."

"Good. I am at your house."

"See you in a few."

*

We all exited the office, and I was locking the building's side door when a bronze Cadillac SUV pulled into the lot.

"That's my wife." Waters said and extended his hand to me. I shook it. He walked to the SUV and got in.

When they drove from the lot, Marcus was behind them in a black unmarked Epsilon Security Service Mustang.

Waters had more faith in the legal system than I did. I understood that people had different experiences with the police. My experiences had not engendered trust or faith. I guessed that Waters being former military police gave him expectations that I didn't have, and I was sure his cousin being a cop gave him some feelings of security. Hopefully, Lee could protect him, but I doubted it. Marcus would stay with him till the end of the day or until he turned himself into police custody.

"You think he is making a mistake?" Carol asked.

"Without a doubt."

Carol was shaking her head no and jingling her car keys in her hand. "Lee can't be trusted, and Waters is trusting him. But there is a God, and She protects babies and fools." She turned from me and walked to her car.

A summer breeze blew through the lot, and the four o'clock sun was still bright and warm; it wasn't blazing, but it was warm enough to be the summer sun. My head hung, and I felt the warmth on the back of my neck. I walked to my car not wanting to hang my head, but it hung.

I was thinking Waters was in trouble, but my anxiety eased thinking of Marcus trailing him, and then I had some decent thoughts about Lee. He did call to tell us the police were involved. He warned us, and it was him that gave Waters my name and Pinkers' name. Maybe Waters and his wife were right; reality was seldom as dark as my thinking.

My plan for exposing the shooter cops was forming. I needed to see to my son, Ricky, and Regina. Then I thought about Regina meeting me at home and my head rose, and I felt a smile spreading across my face, but I needed to see my son first, so I called from the car.

*

I was handing the parking valet twenty bucks to keep my car in the driveway for ten minutes when Chester and Angela walked through glass revolving doors of his high-rise. I held onto my twenty bucks. Chester lived in Hyde Park, and parking close to his building was next to impossible.

"Hey, Dad. I thought you meant later."

He walked to me, and we embraced. He looked like he was wearing his pajamas outside. He had on Tony the Tiger drawstring pants, shower flip-flops, and a very thin wifebeater T-shirt.

"No, I meant now." I handed him the disc from the Asian girl. "Oh, and we learned the names of two other officers that were at Wilson's shooting: Lanham and Harris."

Chester stood erect. "We protested both of their shootings. We marched in front of their homes and at police headquarters. It makes sense that they would be there, damn."

Angela, whose blue jean shorts showed the bottom of her butt cheeks, stepped to his side and put her arm around his waist. Her blouse looked more like a bra than shirt. Neither of them was dressed for outside.

"Chester, I want your editor to clearly identify the shooter on the video. Understand? Make it clear that he opened fire on us first. Understand?"

Chester nodded his head yes and said, "I got you, Dad." He held the disc in his hand and looked down at Angela. "I will take this upstairs now." He turned back to the revolving doors. Angela didn't move, she smiled at me, and I smiled back. Even her smile was familiar to me.

I wanted to ask both of them where they were going, and did they think being outside was safe? But I didn't because it obvious they were headed somewhere before I pulled up, and I remembered Carol saying she had assigned Chester protection.

Chester was paused at the revolving glass doors, and I saw the look of expectation on his face. He was waiting for my protesting question. I didn't give it; instead, I look at Angela and said, "Y'all be safe now, and see you at dinner." I got back into my Benz and drove off.

Chapter Eight

As soon as I turned onto my block, Regina and Sonny were in my line of vision. Regina had Sonny's leash in her hand but not on his collar. He was walking at her side unleashed. A female runner ran up behind them, but the runner gave them a wide berth, running onto a neighbor's lawn. People tended to move out of Sonny's way. My phone rang while I was driving down into the garage. It was Chester. I wasn't expecting a call that soon. Thinking something was wrong, I quickly pressed the call-answer button on my steering wheel.

"Hey, Dad, you've been busy. We just saw you on television. You and one of Norton's social workers."

"Waters, yeah, things are happening."

"Dad, this situation today puts you at the scene of two dead police officers. You are the one that has to be extra careful."

I heard his concern and realized that was the reason for his call. He saw the clip and got scared for his old man. I grinned.

"You and Angela still together?" There was safety in numbers.

"Yep, and her cousin is with us. We were going to meet her at the Metro when you came over. We all agreed to hang out until things get back to normal. That was Mom's suggestion."

"Your mother has been with you today?"

"Yep, before you came by, she had us reach out to Alice."

"Alice?"

"Angela's cousin who is interning at the bank."

The banker threat had eased from my mind.

"Ah, ok. Did you reach your friend about the disc?"

"I did, and it's turning out good. She is editing it now. Hey, Mom says she has a surprise for all of us, tonight - any idea what it is?"

"I will leave that up to her. How long will the editing take?"

"Not long at all. Some of the footage had to be cleaned up a bit."

"All right, see you tonight. And son, stay together, stay in a group – the larger the better. Carol contacted you, right?"

"Yes, and I saw Sean sitting in front of my building. It freaked Angela out when I told her, but after seeing you on television and finding out that the guy who shot Wilson is a cop, she understands."

I got out of the car, closed the overhead garage door with the security pad, disarmed the alarm, and walked into my house.

"About work, can you take a couple of days off?"

He would be safer if he stayed home or at least limited his travel for a couple of days.

"I was starting my two-week vacation on Monday, so things sort of worked out."

He sounded more concerned about the threat than he did earlier, but I still said, "Even though a guard is assigned, I need you stay aware of your surroundings, Chester."

I heard him blow a breath, and I knew he was looking annoyed.

"I will, Dad, but so should you. Don't downplay the danger you are in, please. See you tonight," and he hung up. My son was a man, and he knew me well. Sonny and Regina were entering the house through the front door.

When I got into the kitchen, I saw the table was littered with condominium brochures, but what caught my eye were the pictures of my house. There were external and interior shots. I had the photos in my hand when Regina and Sonny came into the kitchen.

"They look nice, don't they? The photographer was here a short while ago; my agent is putting together a media kit for the house. But even without a kit, she has already set up three walkthroughs for this week: two on Tuesday and one Wednesday morning. I have a cleaning and staging service coming Monday. When they finish, your home will look like a magazine spread."

Regina has always moved fast. She'd probably asked Ricky and Martha to use their home for the wedding. Sonny came to me and rested his head against my thigh. I petted him briskly on the side of his neck and the top of his head.

"He is such a good dog, David. So smart."

Regina's tight jeans displayed her camel toe imprint, and her short sleeved white oxford told me again she was braless. She stepped to me and kissed me on the lips.

"Let's look through the condo kits. Did you call the police?" She walked to blond oak kitchen chair and sat at the matching table.

"Nope." Calling the police was not part of my plan. "I got to show that Redding was a racist assassin, and I have to prove that these other cops were at the scene, and that they were there to kill Wilson as well. I need the city to see the crazy motherfuckers that are in uniform."

Regina heard me, but she was organizing the kits. I was talking to myself anyway... thinking out a plan.

"What are the other names beside Pinker and Redding?"

"Lanham and Harris."

"Sweet Jesus." She looked up from the kit. "Both of them were involved in questionable shootings; I think Harris got acquitted, but he is still suspended. Lanham is still working; no charges were brought against him. You got some real winners here, D."

She placed her eyes in mine. "These men are very dangerous."

"I know, baby."

She returned her attention to the kits, "And oh yes, that Alice girl confirmed what I thought. Theodore Drayman has been purposely removing web information about himself. Alice says he hired a firm to reduce his digital footprint."

I sat at the table across from her. "And she knows this how?"

Regina had the kits stacked in a neat pile. "She is his assistant's intern."

"Still?"

"Yes. She is going to work tomorrow."

"And what is involving you?"

There had to be a story somewhere.

"The lending program. It is blatantly discriminatory. And Drayman is so brass in his target marketing." Her expression changed; it looked like she was smelling rotten potatoes. "He acts as if there is no regulatory oversite. In the memos, he writes 'this is the plan for African American and Hispanics.' It was a memo heading that got Alice's attention, 'Easy Money Zones, African American Neighborhoods.' This guy is precise in his market targets, but he is not original in his thinking.

"History shows the same strategies, the same programming was used against Blacks in the thirties, the forties, the fifties, the sixties, the seventies - up until the current day. Theodore Drayman is following protocol; it appears to be good business to provide high interest loans for older substandard housing with inflated pricing to Black and LatinX people."

Regina was still looking down at the kits, but her tone was crisp with anger. Finding out about the lending program obviously irritated her, but I didn't see why Wilson and his group saw the banker as a threat, so I asked, "And Wilson was protesting this home lending program?"

She pushed the pile of kits to me. "Yes and no. They were in the planning stages. Two demonstrations took place, neither got media coverage, but Alice claims Drayman got nervous because both protests were in front of his building.

"Chester and his group have no real comprehension of the financial damage Drayman's program and those like it have done and are doing to people of color in this country, but Drayman knows, and the last thing he wants are protests. There is freedom in the dark of limited regulation, freedom in operating without the public watching. Wilson brought the public eye with his protest; he didn't know how needed his protests were, but I know.

"What Drayman is doing is a continuation of American oppression on people of color; an attempt at stopping the wealth of Black families. He sees the program as fast profit. But in reality, his fast profit is stolen profit. The program steals the benefits of homeownership from people of color. Equity makes wealth, and his program diverts the equity from the hands of people of color. Drayman's pursuit of fast profit is robbing our community."

That was the Blackest I had ever heard Regina sound. Her sense of community was limited to monied Black people. Her allegiance was to the Black people that lived above the struggles of the poor and the working class. She was akin to Black people who managed wealth from parents, grandparents, and great grandparents. In the past, the Black populace had not been her concern.

She seldom used the terms "us" and "ours" when talking about the problems of the Black community. She was born into a professional family and rarely strayed away from the concerns and beliefs of that status. I couldn't remember her ever saying the word "oppression" before.

She was not raised to see herself as part of the Black populace; she was raised to believe that she was above common Black people, but the oppression of this country changes people. It forces one to look for help, and it forces one to see the safety in numbers. Regina was not the first "I" I saw become a "we" after they witnessed and experienced the institutional racism of this nation. Like many Black Americans living in this country, she must have experienced events that opened her classist eyes. I didn't know what had changed Regina, but her words told me she was changed.

I looked at my beautiful ex-wife slash girlfriend and asked, "So… what are you going to do about it?"

Her eyes rose up from the kits, "Expose him and his program. His actions were easy to follow; the story is practically writing itself. This is Drayman's program, but he has superiors who are aware, and again this type of lending is not new to our community. However, the story is stronger with the information Alice provided. The records she copied will pretty much bury Drayman. My follow-up story will be on the previous attacks, the previous programs used by Grant's Federal Bank on people of color."

She was sitting at the table with me and the pile of kits, but our discussion had placed her mind in the investigative process. She stood and walked from the kitchen to the living area and retrieved her shoulder bag. I wanted to ask her did she consider Drayman a threat to Chester and his friends, but my front doorbell rang.

Sonny walked to the door with me. I checked the video monitor and saw two white men in suits. Sonny sniffed at the bottom of the door and growled. I angled the porch camera to the street and saw their unmarked brown sedan parked in front of my home. I opened the door for the detectives.

"Mr. David Price?" The taller of the two asked. He had on a nice gray light wool summer suit with a crisp gray shirt and white tie.

"Yes."

"If you have a minute sir, we would like to discuss your involvement in an incident with Officer Thomas Pinker."

Their arrival was expected.

"Sure, come on in." I pushed open my screen door.

When we walked into the living area, I noticed Regina had placed her camera phone on the bar facing the couch, loveseat, and my recliner. I walked the detectives to her makeshift recording area, offering them the couch. I sat in my recliner, and Sonny stood alert at my side. Regina sat in the loveseat.

"My wife, Regina Price," I said to the detectives.

The taller, the talkative black-haired one answered, "Good afternoon, Mrs. Price. I am Detective Frost, and this is Detective Beverly." The red-headed Detective Beverly had on a dark blue suit. The material looked thick for summer wear, and dandruff was visible on the shoulders of his suit coat.

Regina nodded her head, returning his greeting with a smile.

"As I stated, Mr. Price, we have some questions concerning an incident with yourself, Officer Pinker, and a Mr. Langston Waters." Detective Frost pulled a small spiral notebook and pen from his tailored gray suit coat pocket.

"Ok," was my answer.

Police in my home was seldom a good thing. My goal was to answer their questions as directly as possible. I gave no open-ended answers.

"Officer Pinker died of a massive heart attack." Frost opened the notebook and clicked the pen.

My empathetic answer was "Sorry to hear that."

Sonny was not panting for breath. I could barely tell he was breathing, and his focus did not leave the detectives on the couch.

The first words Detective Beverly spoke were "Several witnesses place you and Langston Waters with him at his time of death, and others say that you two attended his church's service." He said the words dryly, and he wasn't questioning, so I confirmed his statement.

"All of that is true, Detective."

"Are you a member of Pinker's church?" Frost asked me while surveying the living area. His eyes lingered on the bar. I guessed he was looking at Regina's camera phone.

"No."

"Did you know Officer Pinker prior to his death?" Frost asked.

"No."

"What was the purpose of your meeting?" came from Beverly.

"I wanted to ask him why he was present at Wilson Norton's shooting."

My answer caused them booth to move a bit. Beverly sat straighter, and Frost's left thigh flinched twice.

Beverly asked, "You saw Pinker at Norton's shooting?"

"I did, and he told me officers Alfred Harris, Jeffery Lanham, and Peter Redding were at the scene as well." It was a needed lie, part of my developing plan.

"We know you saw Redding, because you shot and killed him." Beverly declared.

"No. I defended myself against a threat. He was shooting at me." Verbiage is important with any arm of the legal system.

"He died from bullets that came from your gun, security guard." Again, Beverly stated the facts, and he was trying to offend me with the term "security guard," but he didn't know that I considered myself a security guard. I provided a secure environment to my clients, guarding them against danger.

"Can I answer any other questions for you?" I addressed Beverly directly.

A quiet growl came from Sonny.

"You say Harris and Lanham were there yesterday... at the Norton shooting?" Frost asked me.

"According to Pinker."

The detectives looked at each other longer than they intended.

Frost asked me, "How did you know to talk to Pinker?"

"Mr. Waters had his name when he hired me."

"Hired you?" Beverly asked.

"Yes, he felt threatened due to his ward being gunned down on the street by a Chicago police officer."

"Where did Waters get Pinker's name?" Beverly continued ignoring my dig.

"You'd have to ask him."

"Witnesses say you walked away from Pinker while he was having a heart attack." Frost asked the question, but both detectives were looking directly at me.

Sonny's growl became audible.

"Sit." I told him, and he complied. "I thought Pinker fainted," was my truthful answer to Frost's question.

"Why would he faint?" Beverly asked scooting up to the edge of the couch cushion.

"My guess is guilt. I asked him about the kid he dragged off the bus and shot to death, and then he fainted." Another lie, but it caused a pause.

Frost asked, "You didn't think to check him? He was laid out in front of you."

"Honestly... I didn't care."

Beverly motioned to stand. But Frost placed a hand on his shoulder holding him in place.

"So, you left him in the grass to die?" Frost asked.

"I didn't think he was dying. I thought he fainted."

Through clenched teeth, Beverly asked, "Why did Waters draw his pistol?"

"You'd have to ask him that."

"I'm asking you."

"I cannot speak for the man."

"Why would Pinker tell you Harris and Lanham were with him?" came from Frost.

"I have no idea. Maybe *we* should go ask Officers Harris and Lanham why they were there dressed in SWAT attire matching Redding and Pinker."

The detectives restrained themselves from looking at each other.

"What are you insinuating, Mr. Price?" Frost closed his notebook.

"Not a thing. I am just relaying information a Chicago police officer gave me. Are *we* going to speak to officers Lanham and Harris?"

"Good day, Mr. Price." Frost said.

The detectives stood in unison, and Sonny and I walked them to the front door without another word being spoken. They left without a farewell. When we returned to the living area, Regina was at the bar with her phone.

"I think you told them more than they knew."

"I did."

"Why?"

"I think the shooters were acting alone; rogue cops gone crazy."

I didn't know how to tell Regina that her old boyfriend, Detective Johnathan Lee, gave me and Waters the information.

"Gone crazy? Why?"

"Because what was – is no longer. Wilson was organizing protests against police misconduct; that was not supposed to happen. A young Black man was not supposed to be protesting against the police. And he was able to get the media reporting on police actions that were normally hidden.

"And it isn't just Wilson, citizens all over the country are taking pictures with phones capturing police misdeeds. Things are changing faster than those that want to hold on to the past can adjust to. The world is moving past them, and they are losing their minds, going crazy. Attacking Wilson and his organization is those officers reaching back to the past, to a time they understood, but that time is gone, and accepting that fact is driving them crazy."

Regina's phone rang. "It's Chester," she said.

She answered the phone, and I heard him giving her directions.

"What? Wait, do what? YouTube. Ok."

Reinga went to her laptop on the kitchen table with the phone to her ear. I followed her, but Sonny jumped on the couch for a nap.

"Search for what? Wilson's name. Ok." She clicked the phone off and got started on her laptop. Sitting at the table she asked me, "Chester said this is what you requested?" Looking up at me, questioning.

The video started with Wilson's shooting. Chester's voice was narrating; the scene was Redding firing his rifle at Wilson. Chester was heard repeating "Chicago Police Officer Peter Redding" as the shooting replayed three times. The YouTube video blinked, and the scene changed to footage of Redding shooting a man who was on his knees with his hands up. Redding was seen firing his pistol repeatedly, and Chester's voice kept stating, "Chicago Police Officer Peter Redding." The scene with Redding shooting the man was replayed three times with Chester chanting his name.

The scene that ended the video was Wilson protesting in front of police headquarters on the blue milk crate with his bullhorn yelling, "And if this city thinks police violence is acceptable to us, we are here to tell them different! It will not be tolerated, not...by...us! Not... by... us! Not... by... us! Not... by... us!" The video faded to black with Chester chanting, "Chicago Police Officer

Peter Redding, Chicago Police Officer Peter Redding,
Chicago Police Officer Peter Redding."

"Damn," was what Regina said.

I said, "Goddamn," and started laughing with pride.
"Well, if people in the city didn't know Redding was a
police officer, they know now."

"I am not sure this is a good thing." Her words were
weighted with worry.

"It is a good thing. This will inform the public on an
injustice, of an attempted city government cover up."

"It might incite a riot."

"No, it will inform the public."

"Chester is a nurse, an R.N., not an activist."

"It's pretty clear that he is both," I answered.

I was still grinning. Chester and his people had done a
good job. The online exposure was going to be good, but I
needed more.

"No, it's not Chester. It is those people he's with.
Specifically, it is that girl, Angela. Have you noticed that
she always smells like marijuana?"

I had, but I didn't answer.

"She has him thinking with his little head not his big
head. He is thinking with his penis and not his brain. I
watched them today; he is always touching her and
holding her hand and kissing her cheeks and lips. She
can't pass him without him touching her, and whenever
she walks in a room he smiles. It's pathetic. Nope, he is
not thinking with his brain. And did you know she works
at a warehouse? A warehouse.

"Now the other one, the little one, Alice, she just earned an MBA, and she is interning at the bank, and she did her undergraduate work at Spelman and her graduate work at Duke. Her father is a doctor, and her mother has her own real-estate company. But that's not who our son is with, our son's attention is on the warehouse worker."

I offered, "Angela is a very smart and pretty girl."

"Pretty won't get you on the bus and smoking that much marijuana has to affect her intellect. You are too easily impressed, D."

She looked up from the laptop to me. I wrapped my arms around here from the back.

"Calm down. Women have been finding your son attractive for quite a while."

I kissed the back of her neck. She had worked herself into a nervous frenzy. Between the banker and his loan program, Chester's video, the police in my house, and her son dating a woman she didn't approve of, Regina had become flustered.

I wanted to tell her about Lee's involvement in the case, but the time wasn't right. Besides, I had business to get to, a plan to complete. I stood up from the hug.

"I was talking about our son dating beneath his status, not about him being physically attractive."

"Play the video again," I requested.

She restarted the video.

While watching it again, I told her, "I need you to get this into the hands of your television news friends. It would help me if we could get airtime tonight."

"Help with what?"

"Help me eliminate the threat against Chester and myself."

"You are talking about the police threat?"

"I am."

"And you have a plan?"

"I do, and Chester's video gives it lion's claws."

"Ok, I can call in a couple of favors and get it some airtime, but I cannot guarantee tonight."

She closed her laptop.

"When I told Martha, we wanted to use their home for the marriage ceremony, she suggested her preacher. I said no. And telling her no made me realize... I just want it to be us, you and I going to city hall. Do you mind if it's only you and I?" She was looking down at her closed laptop not at me when she asked.

"No Chester?"

"No Chester."

"Just me and you?"

"Just us."

"If that's what you want."

She looked up. "That's what I want. I booked us for 11:30 on August 5th, and we have a four o'clock direct flight to Barbados."

"We do?"

"We do, ten days and nights at an all-inclusive resort."

"Oh. I am impressed."

She stood up from the chair and kissed me.

I put my arms back around her and kissed her again.

"You can tell Chester tonight." She directed.

"I can?"

"Yes, and there is something else you can do for me."

"What?"

"Carry me upstairs and remind me of how much you desire me."

She didn't have to ask twice. We were late getting to Ricky's for dinner.

Chapter Nine

When we pulled up to Ricky's blond brick bungalow, Chester was standing on the porch in blue jeans and a short-sleeved plum polo. He had his phone in his hand, sliding his finger across the screen while talking directly into the device. Regina, in true helpmate fashion, had made some calls and our son's video was being broadcast on two city stations: WGN and WTTW.

Sean, another Epsilon security guard, was parked in front of Ricky's house. He was standing outside another black Epsilon Security Service Mustang, looking like a Bears' linebacker. We nodded at each other. Walking up the stairs, I heard Chester sounding more like a movie producer than an activist or an R.N.

Regina stopped and kissed our son on the cheek before she walked inside the Brown's home. I turned away from Ricky's front door to look at the darkening sky above the lake. I watched small waves moving towards the grassy tree-lined shore of the South Shore Country Club. The evening sky was almost royal blue; the gentle waves, the swaying trees, and even the scattered traffic on South Shore Drive were calming to me. Ricky had a beautiful lake view.

The Brown's living room area had guests. Angela, my son's girlfriend, and her cousin Alice were sitting on a loveseat in front a large set of windows. A slender, balding, bespectacled Dr. Gates and his very shapely wife, Tina, were seating next each other in the center of a long couch. Martha, Ricky's wife, was sitting in an armchair close to Dr. Gates and Tina. Martha looked like the singer Gladys Knight. The two could have been sisters or at the very least first cousins, and Martha could sing as well.

Years ago, when Martha's and Ricky's children were small, there had been no dining room in the house. Martha had torn down the living room and dining room walls and created one large living area. Their children were now adults and residing throughout the Midwest; only Ricky and Martha were in the house, and they entertained regularly, so a dining room table had been added, a regal mango wood table with claw table legs. The table could easily seat ten, and it indicated the dining area.

I followed Martha's lead when I bought my leather couch and love seat. In her large living area, she had two lengthy tan leather couches and two matching loveseats with three studded tan leather armchairs. She forbade Ricky from sitting in the armchairs. The only piece of sitting furniture in the area that was not leather was Ricky's dark brown extra-wide corduroy recliner.

Once their kids were grown and gone, Martha brightened the room with light beige carpet and golden butter walls. One crystal chandelier hung over the dining room table, and another smaller one hung right after the foyer, and she had small spotlights tracking the ceiling and walls. The room was well lit, and I liked it a lot.

The first person that made eye contact with me was Tina, Ricky's other woman. She smiled, stood from the couch, and came to me with an embrace. Her breasts were 44 triple E huge, her hips 56 wide, and her stomach was flat. We hugged, and the woman smelled like cinnamon toast.

She whispered, "See you rolling with the wife again, huh?" Regina had entered behind me. Tina's word reminded me of how long we had been acquaintances. She knew about my life.

"Yeah, we are going at it again."

She ended the embrace, but kept her voice low, "Good for you. Some men should be married; they are better with partners, and you are that type of man."

I was not sure how to respond, so I just smiled. Regina was standing beside me, and she did not know Tina, so I introduced them.

"Regina, this is Tina, Dr. Gates' wife. And Tina, this is my wife, Regina." I dropped the ex. They shook hands, and I quickly beelined over to Ricky sitting in his recliner. When I glanced back at Regina, Martha had joined her and Tina.

"What dey talkin' 'bout?" Ricky asked before I could get seated in an armchair. I guessed that waiting for the dinner had been agitating him all day.

I sat, saying, "Nothing, I just introduced Tina to Regina."

"Yeah, dats right, dey don't know each otda." He was surveying the room like it was a battlefield. "I asked Tina why she didn't tell me 'bout comin' to dinna; she said she didn't see why she should have, and her sneaky ass started gigglin'. Her and Martha already talked about da reunion stuff. I been tryin' to rush da dinner, but everybody is enjoyin' each otdas company. Da young activist gettin' shot by da police is da talk. So, you was dere, shootin' police, huh?"

He was almost laughing when he asked the question.

"I didn't know he was an officer. I was just returning fire," I told him, "It all happened so fast. There was no way I could tell that Redding was the police."

He leaned forward in his chair and towards me. "Be careful, ya don't want ta get yo' brains blown out ova a taillight!" Then he laughed outright, and the mass that was Ricky Brown jiggled in the chair.

"That's not funny."

He was talking about reasons the police could use to stop me: taillights, stop signs, turning signal malfunctions, any traffic violation could get me stopped and killed.

"Yeah it is, and it's true. If it was me, I would stop drivin'."

That did make sense. Driving did give the police access to me. But... Wilson Norton wasn't driving.

"Ya made da Chicago PD's most wanted list. Dey gonna shoot yo' ass fo' jaywalkin'. I don't dink a Black man shot and killed a cop in dis city since '88. Yo' ass is a celebrity. Da streets talkin' 'bout ya. Ya 'bout to get legend status. If da cops kill ya – ya got it; niggas will talk 'bout ya till da end of days."

He pulled his phone from his black linen pants pocket.

"Look at all dese text messages I got from people askin' was dat my buddy. I'm tellin' ya – ya 'bout to be a legend. And now, dey got ya on camera walkin' away from a dyin' cop. Y'all just left him in da grass ta die. Shit man, erbody talkin' 'bout ya. Yous a bad ass nigga, right naw."

I had not thought about how the community looked at our actions because nothing we did was intended to be heroic or publicly shared; we were just moving through the moment.

"Yeah, well, none of that is part of the plan to stop the police from putting holes in me or Chester."

Ricky eased even closer to me. "Ya got a plan?" He was anxious to get involved and that warmed my heart.

"I do. I need to link the other cops to Redding. We got the city seeing Officer Redding as a shooter. I need to shine that same light on the other three."

"Explain."

Ricky was in the dark on the particulars; all he knew of was the police threat.

"Yesterday, there were four cops at the scene, but only one opened fire on us, Redding. Regina's old boyfriend, Detective Lee, saw Pinker there, and he got his name to me. Pinker turned over the other two names after Waters pistol-whipped him."

"Pinker is da cop dat had da heart attack?"

"Yep."

"And Waters was da guy on television wid you. Who is he?"

"One of the social workers that raised Wilson. He was asking questions about me, and Lee put him touch."

"Lee is da cop dat kicked it wid Regina?"

"Yep."

"So da cop, Pinker, he snitched on erbody else afda Waters pistol whipped him?"

"Yep."

"Damn, and da video tellin' erbody dat Reddin' was a cop was part of yo' plan?"

"Yep."

"And Regina's boyfriend got ya in dis shit?"

"Ex-boyfriend. And truthfully, Chester pulled me in. It was because of him that I was there when the cop shot Wilson Norton. They were going to hire us to protect him."

He nodded his afro-sprouting head. "What's yo' next move?"

That was the tricky part.

"I need to link all the cops together and show the city that they were acting together to kill Wilson. And I need to show that Pinker was a racist."

"How ya gonna do all dat?"

"That's why I need you. I need help linking Lanham and Harris to Pinker. I need more information on both of them. I figure bad cops are never bad in just one area."

Ricky tilted his head. "Dats true."

"I need you to look into both of them, see if they are connected to any criminal activity."

"Shit, dat ain't nothin', consider it already done. Two calls should wrap it up. The people on the streets watch crooked-ass cops."

I saw Martha and Regina walking towards us.

"You two get up and come help us set the table," Martha requested.

"'Bout time," Ricky said, standing with huffs and heavy sighs.

Once I was standing, Regina moved closer to me putting her arm around my waist and kissed me on the cheek as we walked into kitchen.

I grabbed the two large platters of catfish from the table and carried them back to the impressive dining room table.

The guests were all seated at the table: Dr. Gates and his wife were side by side with Tina sitting at the end, placing her close to whomever sat at the head of the table. Next to Dr. Gates was Angela, then Chester. Alice was on the other side of the table with three empty chairs. I placed the platters on the table and sat in the chair next to Alice and introduced myself.

"Hey, I'm David, Chester's father."

She had a cherubic round, milk chocolate brown face with dark brown hair. Her hair was styled in the only style I could name, a pageboy, and I could name it because Regina wore one for years when we were married. Alice was so small two of her could have sat in the mango wood high back chair.

"Yes, I know. We have been waiting on you and his mother, Regina Price. She is an investigative reporter, and I have been reading her since high school."

I told the young fan, "I'm sure she will be flattered."

"She was. I told her. We met earlier. She is a nice lady. I never thought I would be a source for her." Alice took a short breath. "And we watched you on television. I thought they should have included you shooting that crooked cop in the video, but Angela edited it out. She said the focus had to be on the cop."

I was surprised. "Angela edited the clip?" When I asked Chester did he have resources to make a video, he didn't say that resource was Angela.

"Yes, she went to school for film production. You didn't know that?"

"I didn't."

"She has a video graphics company, and she's making money."

The table was set, and everyone was sitting. Ricky was at the end with Tina, and Martha was at the end with Chester.

"Do you like interning at the bank?"

"I do, and it is a paid internship. Things are still going well, and they have no idea that I am the leak."

Martha cleared her throat, and we all looked in her direction.

"Thank you all for coming, and if you will bow your heads for grace."

For some reason, I was expecting Angela not to bow her head, but all heads at the table were bowed.

"Lord, it is your mercy that carries us. Amen." Martha was not a long-winded prayer, and I was appreciative because the catfish was smelling good. Alice had referred to herself as the "leak." I watched her pick up the fish platter, take a piece and pass it down. She reached for one of the spaghetti bowls and said, "When I saw the first memo, I was shocked at the language. I knew about target marketing." She took a heaping spoonful of spaghetti. "But not group targeting for exploitation, which is what Drayman is doing. What he is doing is wrong, but I was clueless about what to do. The bank is paying me so well, and the internship is accredited, but I wanted to do something, so I called my protesting cousin, and she knew what to do."

She forked up some fish and closed her eyes while chewing. Martha cooked well. Alice's gaze returned to me. "I started feeling like a secret agent copying the files and everything, and Angela was keeping things a secret with her people. Then they had the protest in front of my work. Seeing it was amazing. I watched with Drayman's assistant out the seventh-floor window."

Regina, who was sitting next to me, asked Alice, "Is that when he, Drayman, called the police?"

She nodded her round brown head in the affirmative. "Yes, he called the police the first time they protested, especially after he had to walk through the protestors to get into the building. He was furious when he got to the office. He was ranting and raving about being connected to the Chicago police force and that they, the protestors, had picked the wrong place to demonstrate. I had to bite the inside of my cheek to stop from laughing."

Chester added, "It was after the bank protest that we started getting specific threat calls."

Angela joined with, "And it was after the bank protest that the fat cop showed up at my job."

"Your job?" Regina asked.

"Yes. I saw him wobbling out of the plant manager's office. It was the policeman that shot the man changing his tire. I remembered his face because he was so fat, and I couldn't understand how someone that large would be a police officer."

She was talking about police Sargent Jeffery Lanham.

"How long ago was this?" Regina was bright-eyed.

"Last week."

"Dat means you two are targets. Dey know ya both." Ricky had four pieces of catfish on his plate; everyone else had one or two.

"It could also mean that more than those officers are involved; identification requires resources. They had help finding out about you," Regina stated. "Drayman's assistant, Elaine Chambers, is that who you work for?" she asked Alice.

"Yes."

"Ok, she scheduled me a 9:45 meeting with Drayman."

"That's an early meeting for him. I will be the one making the coffee." She giggled.

I needed to talk to Lee. Maybe he knew who Drayman's police connections were.

"I would like to go with you tomorrow."

I saw Regina blink at my request, but she smiled and said, "Sure."

Chester was twisting his fork in a mound of spaghetti. He said, "And we have a nine o'clock protest scheduled at the bank tomorrow, too."

Regina asked, "What?"

Chester answered without looking up from his plate. "We will be there as well." He was a grown man making his own decisions. I placed a calming hand on Regina's thigh.

"Do you think that is wise?" she asked Chester.

Ricky Brown added his two cents. "Don't sound smart ta me."

"It's scheduled," was Angela's comment, and she didn't look up from her dinner either. She spoke while chewing.

"What are you saying, Mom?" Chester looked up from his meal, leaving his spaghetti-heavy fork in the center of his plate.

"What I am saying is, this situation, whatever it is, caused your leader and friend to die. Your group's protests have left him in the morgue. Perhaps protesting tomorrow is bit soon. That's what I'm saying." Her words were laden with concern, and her tone was not directive. What she was saying was *please stay your ass home* and that was plain as day to everyone sitting at the table.

"I don't think social change follows a schedule, Mom. If one of us would have been killed Wilson would have continued the protest. We honor him by protesting. There is no honor in standing down," was my son's reply.

Bespectacled Dr. Gates was bald at the crown of his head with nappy hair on the sides and the back of his head. He entered the conversation with, "She's not asking you to stand down; she is suggesting postponing."

All the older people at the table were nodding their heads yes, looking at Chester.

"It is more than Angela and me. Over forty-five people will be involved in the protest. Even if I sat here and agreed not to go, the protest would still take place. Wilson began a movement that has grown beyond us."

Even though I agreed with my son, I asked, "Who is speaking tomorrow?"

"I am," Chester answered.

Regina immediately stood from her seat. "Like hell you are. This is foolishness. Are you insane? That boy was not even protesting when they shot him down." Her words were shrill with excitement, but she was not yelling.

The mother of my son and my son locked eyes. Regina sat back down with her eyes still in his. "Speaking at the protest, going to that protest... is madness, Chester." Concern and fear were heard in her calmer words.

Chester shook his head to the negative. "No, Mother, not madness, but being fed up. And our protesting is working to change what has been. What that bank and institutions like it have done to our community is criminal. What Theodore Drayman has done is criminal. If we don't speak out, if we don't fight back, if we don't express our discontent, if we don't tell him what he is doing is not acceptable, then we are complicit in his oppression of us. We need to tell him his actions are not acceptable, not by us."

Regina lowered her gaze from our son, shaking her head no, but she said nothing. She broke a piece of catfish from the bone and stuck in her mouth with her fingers. She broke off another piece, mashed it together with some spaghetti and stuck that in her mouth as well. She never ate with her fingers in public, never. She was upset.

I looked across the table to Angela and asked, "You are running your own business?" It was my blatant attempt at changing the subject.

Angela was watching Regina fingering the food, so she seemed a little startled by my question. "Um, yes, for about four years since I graduated."

We looked at each other and smiled. "And I hear it is profitable?" I added.

Tina answered my question with, "It is. She paid us back her start-up loan after her second year in business. She has her father's head for money."

Dr. Gates started coughing and choking on his food. Tina had to pat him on the back. "Are you ok, Ernest?"

He cleared his throat and drank down half a glass of lemonade nonstop.

"I'm fine, baby; something went down the wrong pipe."

I thought a dentist saying "the wrong pipe" was funny, and I quietly chuckled. Regina stopped eating altogether, and she was looking from Angela to Ricky with a curious expression on her face. To me she whispered, "Is it me, or does that girl have Ricky's nose, mouth, and eyes? She looks just like Ricky."

I looked, and it was true. I hadn't noticed how much Angela resembled Ricky... they looked a hell of a lot alike. And why Angela looked familiar to me became very clear. She looked just like Ricky's mother. "Damn," I said unintentionally.

I started wishing Regina had a bigger piece of fish on her plate to occupy her wandering eyes.

"You know, we are all cousins," was what I whispered to her.

Ricky never mentioned Tina being pregnant with his child, but he did hook her up with Dr. Gates. Angela being Ricky's daughter was a crazy thought, and I tried to push it out of my mind because there were enough thoughts running around inside my head.

Dr. Gates, who had regained composure, said, "I really wish you both would reconsider attending tomorrow's demonstration. You both have so much more to consider with the baby coming. Your health issues don't need the stress, Angela."

He turned his head to face my son and said, "And Chester, that child will need a father, not a martyr. I don't mean to be cruel, but family responsibilities trump fighting for social justice. You have real-life duties. Let someone else give that speech tomorrow."

Regina grabbed my thigh. "Hold it. What did he just say?" she asked, looking at me.

I answered, "I think he said our son is expecting."

"No, he could not have said that because our son would have told us if he was expecting a child." She was digging her nails into my thigh and talking to me and staring at me.

Chester who was sitting across the table from her and me said, "Wow."

It was Angela's turn to stand from the table. "Dag, Daddy. We were going to tell them later this evening, and we are both aware of our responsibilities." She stepped back from her chair and pushed it to the table.

"You don't talk to you father like that, young lady." Tina appeared to be ready to rise from the table as well.

"Angela, neither you nor Chester are acting like responsible adults," Dr. Gates continued.

The only people at the table still eating were Ricky and Alice. Chester stood as well and pushed his chair to the table.

"Where are you two going?" Regina queried.

"Thank you for dinner, Aunt Martha," Chester said, smiling at Martha. I had to admire the calm he was projecting. He told his mother, "I will call you later tonight. I love you." He was talking like a man who paid his own bills and came and went like he wanted.

Regina tightened her grip my thigh and said, "I love you too, son. We will talk tonight."

Alice hurriedly put another forkful into her mouth and stood from the table, and she joined the leaving couple.

"Well, I hope that made you happy, Ernest," Tina said to Dr. Gates.

"Things should be in the open. We are all about to be family." Dr. Gates picked up his fork and returned to the catfish.

I did the same, and Regina reached for the platter of catfish and got herself another piece. A lot was going on with those of us sitting at that table, but we all avoided eye contact, and it seemed like everyone was finished talking, and all our attention went back to the meal.

"Dey ain't kids," Ricky said.

"And they have their own money," I said.

"And good jobs," Tina added.

"And they're educated," Dr. Gates said. "We can assume the decision to keep that child was not made haphazardly."

"But they are not married," Martha said.

"Not yet," Tina said. "Have you seen how they look at each other? They are really in love." And she and Martha shared smiles.

Regina's stomach grumbled and she belched.

"Please excuse me."

*

After the caramel cake and orange sherbet desert, Dr. Gates asked Ricky, "Do you mind if I have word with you on the porch?"

That question got the attention of everyone sitting at the table, especially Tina.

"'Bout my teeth or somethin'? My bill should be paid." Despite asking a question, Ricky didn't look curious. He had a blank poker player's expression on his face.

"No, it is another private matter." Dr. Gates cleared his throat and scooted his chair back.

I wanted to hear what was going to be discussed, and Tina looked as curious as I felt.

"I'm tired," Regina told me. "I'm ready to go home."

I was ready to go too, especially after eating like I did, but there was no way my nosy nature was going to let me leave without knowing what Dr. Gates wanted to talk about. "Ok, let's just wait until they go out and talk. When they come back in, we can leave."

She leaned over and kissed me on the cheek. "Ok, I am going to help Martha clean up." She got up with Martha and Tina, and the three started gathering bowls and saucers.

Dr. Gates didn't wait for Ricky to agree to talk. He stood from the table waiting for Ricky to stand. When Ricky didn't move, he walked to the porch anyway. Ricky signaled me to join them with a tilt of his head. I didn't hesitate to stand and follow them out.

It was dark out, and the amber streetlight along with Ricky's porch light illuminated the area. Dr. Gates gave me a querying look, which I ignored, and sat on the top porch ledge.

Ricky sat on the other top ledge and told Dr. Gates, "Speak freely. I have no secrets from D."

I gazed out onto the street. Moments passed, and I could feel a standing Dr. Gates considering the situation.

He began with, "I told Tina before we were married that I was born sterile. Her having Angela eight months after we married was not a shock, but a blessing, because I wanted to be a father. I never asked about the biological father, never." He pulled an envelope from his pocket and handed to Ricky. "Angela has a bleeding condition that was easily manageable through her childhood, but as a pregnant woman, she will need a blood match from a genetically matching donor with the same blood type. Her mother doesn't have the blood type. You, her father, do."

"What is ya' talkin' 'bout?"

"I'm talking about you saving my daughter's life. She will need blood from you after she births her child."

"Why ya' dink I'm her daddy?"

"I don't think, I know. Read the report. I took several genetic samples from you over the years, but the need to confront you with the truth never presented itself. What we require is your blood a week before the delivery. You are an exact match."

"What did Tina say?" Ricky's question was asked defensively.

"We have never discussed it. Angela knows of the illness, but not that you are her match. I made the decision to approach you on my own."

Ricky Brown would be a grandfather of my grandchild. There was no doubt in my mind that he would give the blood.

Ricky said, "I ain't got a problem wid none of it."

Dr. Gates continued with, "And I would appreciate your discretion in this matter. I see no gain in anyone knowing your genetic association with Angela."

Sitting on the ledge, I was wishing I hadn't come out on the porch. I needed another situation in my mind like I needed a toothache.

Then the three us heard, "You see ladies, that right there... is some controlling male bullshit."

Our heads turned to the door, and we saw Tina, Martha, and Regina standing behind the screen door. Tina was speaking. "I birthed the child. I carried her in my body for close to nine months, and this man thinks he should decide what I should know about my child, and what my child should know about her father. And Ricky, how are you just going to sit there and let him babble on like that?"

Yep, I was ready to go.

"Tell him the truth, Ricky Brown. Tell him you have been giving Angela blood since she was twelve years old. Tell him."

No one was yelling, but I felt like the screaming was sure to come. I did not know who knew what, and I didn't want to find out.

"Look-a-here, dis situation gettin' outta control. What da hell goin' on wid you, Tina?" If Ricky had been a hundred pounds lighter, he might have jumped up to add emphasis to his word. But his weight only allowed him to squirm on the ledge.

Tina opened the door and step out onto the porch and said, "This is what's going on with me, Ricky Brown. I am tired of a twenty-eight-year-old bullshit secret; well, half a fucking secret. You two motherfuckers is the problem. Hell, I slept with both of you. Get the fuck over it. Angela is Ricky Brown's biological child, and Ernest, you knew I was pregnant when you married me. This super-secret shit is crazy. Angela is old enough and smart enough to handle the truth. Hell, everybody else involves knows. We got to tell her."

Her tirade silenced the group.

"Let's all come back inside and talk," Martha said.

I guessed Martha was part of the everybody knowing. Tina must have gotten pregnant before Martha and Ricky got married. Yep, that would explain her threatening to trash the wedding. Decades-old situations were being discussed, and it was way more information than I wanted inside my head. There was no way I was going back into the house. However, Regina beat me to the exit punch.

"Martha, I can't. I really need to prepare for my meeting with the banker in the morning." She stepped from behind the screen door and began walking down the stairs, and I followed.

Once we were down the steps, I didn't look back, because the Browns and the Gates were more than capable of handling the situation.

Chapter Ten

There were more than forty-five people at the morning protest, a lot more. Regina and I had to "excuse me" and "pardon us please" through the loud crowd to get to the bank door. Looking through the boisterous protestors, I did not see Chester or Angela.

Inside the bank, Regina took the lead walking through the vast bank lobby to a very tall, very wide, white man with purple spiked hair. He was standing under the hanging "Information" sign at a podium-like desk in the middle of the theater-sized lobby.

"We have a 9:45 appointment with Mr. Drayman."

"Your names?" The huge man asked.

"Regna and David Price."

Hearing her state our names made me smile. I seldom heard her say the name, Price. Regina never dropped my last name largely because she reached her reporter status with the name Regina Price.

After the information giant finished on the computer, he handed us lapel sticker labels and pointed to the bank elevators to his left. "Those will take you to seven. Have a pleasant day." He looked from us to the windows that showed the protesting crowd outside the bank. The expression on his face was worried, almost fearful. We walked to the elevators.

"I didn't see Chester out there, did you?" Regina asked stepping into bronze antique lighted elevator car.

"I didn't see him or Angela, and I searched the crowd."

She pushed seven; her choices went to twelve. "Maybe he listened to me."

I doubted that; he was probably in his car reviewing his speech. The elevator was silent while rising, almost motionless. I was surprised when the doors opened so quickly on seven. What surprised me more was seeing the Pillsbury Doughboy face of Jeffery Lanham.

An older white man, who I guessed was Drayman, was yelling at him, which resulted in Lanham being peppered with spittle. The screaming older man had strange orange, gray, and blondish hair. His stomach hung over his belt, and he looked like he was threatening a heart attack at any moment.

"What the fuck! How hard could it be to stop a group of nig… Black people from protesting on a downtown street? This is fucking Chicago, and you are the fucking police! Get those idiots gone, or you will be gone. Understand me? Get it fucking done!" Drayman turned and walked away, and Lanham turned away as well, and his redirection had him looking directly at us. Recognition showed in his raised eyebrows. He knew who I was.

He walked by us in his white police sergeant's uniform shirt without slowing; he pushed the elevator button with his back to us. From our ascent, the car was still there, and the doors opened immediately. Lanham stepped on the elevator, and we stepped to the desk where an older woman with silver hair pulled into a bun was sitting.

Regina asked, "Elaine Chambers?"

"Good morning, Ms. Price. Mr. Drayman will be with you shortly." We all acted as if we didn't just witness the rude outburst. The office door behind secretary's desk was slammed closed, and Drayman could still be heard cursing to high heaven.

"Please take a seat." The silver haired receptionist opened her wrinkled pink hand to a sky-blue faux leather couch on the other side of a marble tiled coffee table. Regina and I walked to it and sat.

The sun was beaming through a large window to our left, and I was fighting the impulse to go to it and scan the crowd below for Chester.

Regina obviously shared the same desire because she said, "Sit still. We will find out soon enough."

Alice appeared from behind us carrying a silver tray which was holding a black coffee pitcher, four mugs, a small bowl of cream and a little black box sugar holder. She was dressed like Carol in a pastel pink two-piece business suit with a white high collar blouse She did not acknowledge us, walking through the sun's beams, and we kept the same clandestine demeanor. She walked beyond the secretary's desk and tapped on the door Drayman had slammed.

"Enter." He barked.

She pushed the door open and left it open as she placed the tray on a small table. Alice made an immediate about-face, leaving Drayman's office door ajar. She gave us a slight smile when she passed and returned to wherever she came from.

"Send in the reporter," Drayman snapped out to his assistant.

Seeing fat ass Sargent Lanham gave me the information I came for. The two were connected – the banker and the cops. My efforts had to be focused on connecting the ends, but I stood when Regina stood and followed her past the receptionist's desk into the office.

When Drayman glared up from his desk and saw the two of us standing there, his confusion was apparent.

"It takes two of you to interview me about a mortgage program?" The pudgy man with rosy cheeks and ears asked. His red and black striped tie was loosened, and perspiration marks were present under both arms of his white shirt.

Regina chuckled. "I contacted you, but the story has many contributors." She opened her portfolio and pulled out the memo that read – 'Easy money zones, African American neighborhoods.' "It was a team investigation that uncovered this memo." She placed the memo on his desk, and Drayman picked it up.

I was glad that I had followed Regina's lead and suited up for the meeting. She had on a blue pinstriped pants suit with a grey blouse, and I was in my only Brooks Brothers; it was dark blue, almost black, and I had on a grey shirt too with a grey tie in a Windsor knot.

"This is an interoffice memo; it isn't meant for public distribution. Sales memos often have harsh headers."

Regina nodded her head in the affirmative. "Yes, I can imagine. But for my own information Mr. Drayman, what makes African American neighborhoods easy money?" Regina still hadn't sat, and Drayman hadn't offered a seat.

His eyelids begin to flicker after Regina's question. He answered, "Easy money is a sales expression."

I saw Regina's thin lips pressing together. "Oh. I was mistaken. I thought you used the term because your bank made high interest loans easier for African Americans and LatinXs to qualify for. I thought the term was used because inflated home values justified lenient lending policies in Black and LatinX neighborhoods."

His eyelids continued blinking as he asked, "What?"

"Yes, I figured when high interest loans were given on inflated home prices, foreclosures were sure to follow, returning homes to institutions to resell, leaving the one-time homeowner in enough debt to destroy her or his family. I thought that was what the term 'easy money' meant.

"But you might be right – it could merely be a harsh sales term, easy money. But you know... it does make a good article title too."

Regina pulled a draft of her article from her portfolio. It was titled, "Easy Money."

"You have until end of business today to respond. We go to press tonight."

Regina faced me and nodded her head toward the open office door, and we walked out of Drayman's office. The assistant did not turn her head from the computer screen as we walked by her. At the elevator, I pushed the down button, and the doors opened before I could release a much-needed exhale.

"Are you really going to press with the story?"

"It's done. I put it to bed last night. He won't have anything to say. The truth is too damning. He isn't the first banker to act so egregiously, and I am not the first reporter to report on this type of attack, and I won't be the last.

"What Drayman is doing here in Chicago is being done all across the country and not to just LatinX and Black people – poor people of every ethnicity are falling victim to these institutions, so much so that reporters have given it a name, predatory lending." The elevator moved just as hush on its descent, but there was no quiet outside the bank.

*

Our son, Chester, was not on a milk crate, but he had a bullhorn in his hand walking through the crowd, and there were two hundred plus protesters. I spotted M&M flanking him to the left and right. M&M stood for Mitchell and Michael, two of my best security escorts.

The chant Chester leading was, "Save our homes! Save our lives! Save our homes! Save our lives!" Protesters were stabbing the air with a picture poster of Drayman behind bars. A bus pulled up and more protestors piled out with signs. The crowd was pulsating with the chant, "Save our homes! Save our lives! Save our homes! Save our lives!"

Every local station in the city had cameras on the scene. Wilson's death had obviously got his organization more media coverage. I was watching Chester when a microphone was shoved in my face, "Why are you out here?" the aggressive young Black male reporter asked me.

"Injustice has to stop. We need justice," was my sincere, knee-jerk answer. I was thinking about the bank's loan program.

Then the reporter shook me with, "Is that why you shot down Officer Redding, for justice?"

How did he know I shot Redding? I didn't recognize the young brother, but I answered, "No, not at all... that was self-defense."

He continued with, "Have you seen the video released by the city? It does not look like self-defense. You are seen taking aim and firing your pistol."

I was confused. I had been edited out of Chester's video. I answered, "No, I have not seen the video."

Regina pulled me away from the reporter and the cameraman saying, "We have no further comment."

Steps away from the protesters and the reporter Regina said, "The city is hitting back in response to Chester's video. They have released a video. They are trying to change the narrative. They want the attention on you instead Redding." Other reporters and cameramen were coming our way. "We have to go."

We'd taken a cab downtown, so Regina hailed another. The yellow sedan stopped, and we hopped in. I gave the woman driver Ricky's address to avoid possible media at my house or Regina's.

"This is getting crazy," I said, looking back at the reporters and cameramen we left behind. My phone rang and the screen read, 'asshole.' It was Detective Lee. I answered the call.

"We need to meet, now."

What was it with Lee giving me orders? Instead of saying, go fuck yourself, I said, "Ok, thirty minutes, 6928 S. South Shore Drive." I gave him Ricky's address as well. We ended the call simultaneously.

The time had come to tell Regina about Lee's involvement in the case. "Did I tell you that it was Detective Lee that put me in touch with Langston Waters?" I hadn't, but the question seemed like a good way to start a difficult conversation.

She was going through her phone, not looking at me. "No, he did. Was that him on the phone? The video must be damning; it is trending all over my sources."

She said Lee told her about his involvement. Did I hear her wrong? "Yep, that was him."

"He is meeting us at Ricky's?" She asked still searching her phone.

"Yep."

"Good, he will have insight into what the police are planning." She hadn't looked up.

I was feeling some-kind-a-way about how nonchalantly she said they talked on the phone. "So, you and Lee are still talking?"

I looked past her and out the window on her side of the taxi.

"Yes, of course. We are still very civil with each other. He is a good source of information from time to time." She stopped checking her phone and cocked her head to me. "Wait... are you jealous?" She started grinning from ear to ear, and that made me smile.

"No, not really. I was just worried about telling you he was involved in the case, but you already know, so..."

Going back to her phone, she said, "Yeah, he called me when Waters called him, and he asked did I think you would mind if he gave Waters your number. I told him no."

The cab driver quickly looked back at me and said, "I saw you on TV this morning." She snickered and turned back around. "And that was you they showed yesterday leaving that cop in the grass having a heart attack." She shook her head causing the beads on her cornrows to rattle. "What do you do for a living?"

It was an honest question, and I had to laugh at her candor.

"I run a protection service."

She shook her head again causing her beads to rattle. "Really, you sho' ain't protecting these cops out here that's for damn sure. I prayed for you this morning, brother, you and your partner. These police ain't nothing to play with. You be careful."

My partner, she was talking about Waters. We probably did look like partners on the video clip. I would get updated on his status from Lee.

Regina reached over and put her hand on my knee. "She's right. They have placed a target on your back."

*

Ricky, Lee, and Dixon were on Ricky's porch when we pulled up in the cab. Ricky was standing on his porch above the detectives. Lee was sitting on one of the lower porch ledges and Dixon was sitting on the other. I was wondering was Lee going to hug Regina with his greeting. He didn't. They simply nodded their heads at each other.

"So, your kid is the number two man in Wilson's Norton organization?" Lee asked me.

"I don't know his rank. Why are you asking?"

Dixon growled out his answer. "Because the name Price is buzzing through the whole damn city. You and your son are generating plenty of conversations with the brothers in blue: him and his video, and you and your video. You two are celebrities." There was no humor in the gruff tone of his words.

Regina and I were standing in the sun at the foot of Ricky's porch stairs. I was next to Dixon, and she was next to Lee. Ricky never let the police into his home unless they came with a warrant, and when the police had a warrant, they were met on the porch by lawyers. His attorneys were politically and judicially connected, and they were informed when warrants concerning Ricky Brown were issued.

On the streets, Ricky Brown was a nefarious crime boss, and among the city's legitimate businessmen, he was a respected peer. He had never gone to prison, much to the regret of retired and active Chicago police and FBI agents. He was on both of their most hated lists, and truth was... he hated them with equal animosity and power.

Ricky Brown was extremely wealthy, and he used his wealth to protect himself. I had the detectives meet me at his house because I didn't trust Lee or Dixon. At my home, they might have set me up for an arrest or an accidental police shooting. Bringing them to Ricky's was safer because he always had at least three bodyguards watching his house, and he had security cameras surveying his entire property.

Lee told me, "My cousin was released this morning with no charges filed, and I drove him and his family to the airport. They are all going to Quebec for a month. He wanted me to tell you that."

"Thank you. I'll call him later."

"Do that, and you might want to consider a little family vacation yourself."

Again, it sounded more like he was giving me an order more than offering advice.

"Nope, not a good time: my wife is in the middle of a career-changing case, and I have been hired to protect the city's most noted activist, Chester Price." I hadn't planned on putting emphasis on "my wife," the words just came out that way.

Dixon stood from the porch ledge seat. "This is not a joke, security guard. This warning, us telling you to leave town for a minute, is us doing your ass a favor. Alfred Harris was called back to active duty and named SWAT Commander. He was second in command, but now he's the head, and you know who he named his second?"

I said, "Jeffery Lanham."

"You got it, smart guy. And you know what unit is called for social unrest, right? The next time your kid protests, you might as well call the funeral home."

Regina instantly moved between Dixon and me and wrapped me in her arms. Her movement was stopped by reflex attack. Dixon had threatened my son.

"Get da fuck off my property," came from Ricky.

Lee stood and told me, "You need to know this. Last week, SWAT raided a group of political radicals and claimed to find only two handguns, but the tip that came in reported automatic rifles on location. I'm thinking they found those automatic rifles, but they have a different use for the firearms. Understand me?" He retrieved his car keys from his suit pants pocket and opened the brown Ford sedan remotely. He and Dixon left the porch and got into the car without another word.

Regina and I climbed the steps to Ricky.

"What other use?" Regina asked me. "For the weapons, what other use would they have in mind?"

I didn't want to scare her, but I wanted her informed. "Framing Chester and his people. Placing the rifles at a location before or after the police shoot the place up."

She stood statue still on the porch. "Wait, you mean like Chester's apartment? They would plant weapons there and shoot up the place?"

"Or any place that the group meets. Norton's would be my first guess."

She stood silent looking out to South Shore Drive. The reality of the situation was gagging her.

Ricky said, "Ya know what crossed my mind dis mornin', D.?"

I wanted to say something to soothe Regina's worried look, so I didn't answer his question.

"Me and you is gonna be grand Pappy to da same baby. Ain't dat somedin'."

His words made me smile, but not Regina. She turned from facing the street and the lake to Ricky's front door; she opened it and entered the home.

"Where y'all comin' from?" Ricky asked me.

"The bank. Regina had a meeting with a VP that is cheating Black and LatinX people with high interest rate loans."

"Why did you go?"

"Because the banker is linked to these shooter cops."

"Dat's hard to believe. Rich people ain't got no time fo' racist ass cops."

I opened the door and walked inside without answering him. He was ignoring the fact the police have been the centurions for the rich since the hatching of Western civilization.

Martha was sitting at the dining room table with ledger-type documents in front of her. It was Martha who got Ricky into legitimate businesses. He would have remained a southside crime boss had not her vision made him see a bigger picture. Regina walked directly to Martha and sat at the table with her. Ricky took his easy chair, and I sat in the armchair next to him.

He picked up the remote. "I recorded da video." He turned on wall mounted television, and the clip started with me aiming my pistol at Redding and firing. The rifle was seen flying from his hand, and I was still firing. He was shot in the head, and I was still firing until he fell back to the sidewalk. They had edited the video - it looked like I shot him down, not like I was returning fire.

"Damn, if I only saw that... I would think I killed him in cold blood." Seeing the tape explained why the whole city thought I unjustly killed Redding, and I understood why officers would be gunning for me. "I look like a cop killer."

Ricky offered, "Dats cause ya is a cop killa. Ya killed a cop."

I stood up and took a couple of aimless steps. "They are using the media the way I planned on using the media. I was hoping to rile up Black folks and progressives; they are hoping to rile up the police and the right. I will have to be aware of police loving right wingers and the actual police."

Martha asked, "How badly was it edited?"

I sat back down in the chair. "A lot. The situation started when Redding shot and killed Norton. I shot him after he shot Norton and continued shooting at us. All of that is edited out."

Martha asked, "Is that why the police haven't arrested you, because they know the tape was edited, and the shooting was legal?"

Regina added, "Legal does not matter in the court of public opinion, and the public only focuses on one event at a time. Instead of having the public's attention on Redding shooting Norton, they shifted the public's gaze onto David."

Martha asked Regina, "What "they" are you speaking of?"

Regina placed her palms down on the table. "Now... that is the million-dollar question. My initial thought was City Hall, but we had a cop in a banker's office, and that made me think corporate interest, but we have a cop placed on disciplinary leave returning to work with a promotion, and that indicates the city again. Whoever the actual "they" is – they are powerful and still a mystery to me."

I agreed with her. "And this means they can place a shooter cop at the head of SWAT."

"What do you mean, shooter cop?" Martha asked.

Ricky answered, "Da cop, Harris, was da policeman dat killed Reverend Baker's son."

Martha jerked in her chair. "Ooh my God, that man refused to apologize or even admit he made a mistake. He kept saying, 'I told the boy to stop, and he kept running.' He said that over and over, trying to make running away a reason to shoot someone eight times in the head and back. No, not that man, he should not be getting promoted, and especially not to SWAT. Dear Lord, the whole city knows he is evil. Who would promote him?"

Regina answered, "People who think Black lives don't matter." She pulled her bag from her shoulder and retrieved her laptop and placed it on the dining room table.

"Dats a lot of people. Y'all ain't really thankin' it is one person or a group of people behind all dis mess – is you? No way. Da banker and da activist ain't got nothin' ta do wid each oda. Dem racist ass cops shootin' Black people ain't got nothin' to do wid banks cheatin' Blacks and Mexicans."

Ricky was missing the point. "But it does," I said. "Because banks and the police see us the same; they see us as animals whose lives don't matter. Harris didn't see a person running away; he saw a Black boy running away, and in his mind, it was ok to shoot a Black boy eight times in the back and head. Drayman doesn't see families; he sees Black people that can be cheated. So, you are right, there are a lot of people who think Black lives don't matter. But something in my thinking is telling me these shooter cops, Pinker, Lanham, Harris, Redding, and the banker Drayman, are all connected. Yeah, institutional racism is prevalent throughout the country, there is no arguing that, but this situation is linked. Somebody we can put our hands on is behind all this bullshit. I know it. I can feel it."

I think I was the only one in the room that believed what I said, because no was looking at me. Regina was on her laptop, and Ricky was replaying the video with Martha watching. I sat and watched the video again too.

When the clip stopped, Ricky tapped me on the knee, and he lowered his voice, "I bought yo' boy Lanham's debt last night. He owed Ned-the-Bookie fifty large. Ned sold me the debt for fifteen; now I understand why. He thought Lanham was gonna to walk away from da debt wid da new SWAT job. Ned called him and told him da debt was sold, and he set a meetin' wid da fat cop fo' six tonight."

Lanham was fatter than Ricky, but not by much.

"Da oda one, Harris, got a regular thang goin' on wid White Helen."

I hadn't heard that name in over twenty years, White Helen aka Helen Swift. "Man, she's still around?" White Helen had to be sixty-plus years old. She was a veteran prostitute when Ricky and I were in our twenties.

"Yep, and workin' her place on the regular. Her joint is kinda high-class. She brought a Benz like yours, only silver. She sees Harris at seven in da mornin' every Tuesday. She said he proposed to her last week. He told her was gettin' a new job, a professional position dat would require him to have a wife."

I couldn't picture a fifty or sixty-year-old White Helen in my mind. The memory of her youthful image was all I could see. "Really? What did she say to his proposal?"

"She said yeah. But sayin' and doin' is two different dangs. I'm thinkin' we approach him afta his regular visit. Get him comin' out of her place in da mornin'."

"Yeah, tomorrow would be best. The sooner we meet him the better."

"Ya got it."

A new plan was birthing. The media plan was dead in the water. Forced introductions were power moves, gangster moves, Ricky Brown moves. These cops needed to know that my son had protection, and that I wasn't afraid of them.

"Where yo' car?"

"I left it at Regina's. We took a cab to the bank."

"Look-a-here, I was goin' over to Chester's to see Angela. You want to ride wid me?"

Before I can answer, we heard a joint, "I'm going too," from Regina and Martha. If they heard Ricky asking me to ride with him that meant they heard all the other planning as well, and they hadn't said a word.

Ricky grinned at me and told the women, "Awight, dats cool wid me. Let's ride."

I told him, "I want to stop and pick up Sonny to leave him with Chester."

"Cool, dat mut should fit in da back of Martha's Lexus."

My thinking was that Sonny would provide another shield of protection between our foes and my son.

*

Ricky and I were in our early twenties when we got to know White Helen intimately. As young men, we prided ourselves on "getting chose." We knew women picked, "chose," guys they wanted to have sex with; and we were both getting chose regularly. Paying for sex was not part of our reality, but... Ricky did pay for White Helen's favors, initially. It was her pimp, Steady Freddy, who convinced him that buying her affections was a "player's" move.

One sunny afternoon, we were at Foster Park, and I was admiring the '76 canary yellow Eldorado Biarritz Ricky had just bought. Ricky had to take it "as-is" due to his negotiated price. While he was going over the car, he discovered a very small tear in the white convertible roof, and we were discussing repair options.

"Buy a new top," was my suggestion.

"I got fifty-three cents left ta my name, D. Dat ain't gonna happen."

"Ok, you could put a little piece of duct tape on it until you get your money up. They make white duct tape, and it's just a little rip. Ain't nobody going to notice the duct tape. Put a little thumb-size piece on the inside and the outside."

He was nodding his head yes to the duct tape suggestion when Steady Freddy pulled up on us in a black '78 Corvette. My attention shifted from Ricky's Eldorado to Steady Freddy's Corvette.

Steady Freddy parked behind Ricky's Eldog and got out of the Vette barefooted. He was dressed in a lime green jumpsuit with over ten gold ropes and chains around his neck. His curly brown hair was around his shoulders and down his back. We all thought he was Puerto Rican, but Steady Freddy claimed to be Pottawatomie and Jamaican, but he walked, talked, and hustled like us. He was five to seven to years older than me and Ricky, and he was the richest pimp we knew.

"What it be like, young players? Y'all out here looking good." He stood next to the Eldorado grinning with his four gold-capped front teeth reflecting the sun. He had diamonds on each index finger and pinky, and each of his ears had three holes with fat diamond studs in them.

Ricky and I stood up a bit straighter and leaned toward Steady Freddy a bit. We were anxious to hear what he had say. Steady Freddy was a meteor in our world – he blazed by us aflame in gold, diamonds, and tailor-made clothes, and he always drove the finest automobiles. He seldom said three words to us, so him stopping got our attention.

He looked us up and down and then wagged his manicured index finger. "I am under the impression that neither of you young players has ever had... some white girl pussy." He pressed fat lips together and shook his head to the negative.

My eyebrows went up because I hadn't. I didn't think it was something I was supposed to have done. But the tone Steady Freddy spoke in made it sound like sex with a white woman was an expected thing for a "player" to do.

Before that conversation with Steady Freddy, when I thought about sex and white women, I remembered the picture of Emmett Till's beaten corpse in his casket, and I remembered the stories of Black men being lynched, skinned, and burned alive because of associating with white women. No, having sex with a white woman was not a desire of mine.

"Am I right?" Steady Freddy asked looking each of us in the face. "Tssk, tssk, tssk." He shook his head again from left to right several times. "What type of player ain't never had no white girl pussy? Every real player has been all up in the pink pussy, but I can look in each of your faces and tell y'all ain't been in a pink pussy."

I wanted to ask why was having a sex with a white girl important, but it was Steady Freddy talking, so I didn't ask, I just listened.

"As a player, a true player, you should always be going against the grain. Squares go along to get along, but players break the rules, and we experience all of life's pleasure. Neither one of you knows the tenderness of a white girl. Neither one of you has felt the silkiness of white-girl hair or the soft smoothness of white-girl skin. Helen! Get your pretty white ass out of that car, hoe."

White Helen got out of the Vette dressed in a black leather fishnet bikini that matched her jet-black hair and large black areolas and thick black nipples that were displayed through cut outs in the bikini top.

"Y'all need to experience why the white man will kill you for getting some of this pussy. Whitey don't protect nothing like he protects white pussy. Don't you want to find out why?"

I didn't, and him saying the "white man will kill you" brought a lynching image to the forefront of my mind. I saw an angry white mob pointing to a Black man's body swinging from a tree.

To White Helen, Steady Freddy said, "Turn around hoe and show these players that plump pink ass." She turned around and stopped with her ass facing us; her hips were wide, and her butt protruded out.

"Damn," was how Ricky replied. I remained silent and confused. Two emotions filled my head: fear and lust. Any shapely woman in a fishnet bikini would have been the object of my desire, but looking at Helen's wide protruding pink ass felt wrong. I wanted to close my eyes or look away, but I didn't. I had never seen a white girl with a big ass, so I stared.

Steady Freddy said, "I know. Y'all heard white girls didn't have ass, but you see the truth right here." He slapped White Helen on the left butt cheek and told her, "Get back in the car, hoe" and she complied while looking back over her shoulder smiling at Ricky.

To us, Steady Freddy said, "Now young players. I just got me an apartment right across the street, and the white hoe, Helen, will be working there twenty-four hours a day. Step up your game and come get some of what the white man tells you not to touch. Pussy Cat is one the doorbell." He grinned at us like the confident salesman he was, and that was our introduction to White Helen. I was glad when he drove off.

"She got a big ass," Ricky said watching the Vette drive away.

Chapter Eleven

One of Ricky Brown's workers drove us to Chester's in Martha's pearl white Lexus 450. The driver pulled us up to the luxury condominium's revolving doors.

He told Ricky, "Sir, if you call me a minute or so before you come down, I will be right here."

Ricky replied, "Cool," as we piled out of the Lexus.

Sonny was heeling at my side as we walked through the polished stone walled lobby. The guard at the greeting desk recognized Regina and me and nodded us by. The elevator in Chester's building reminded me of the one in the banker's building. The same antique lighting was present. Regina pushed nine; she had a choice of ten.

Martha, who had been quiet most of the ride from their house to Chester's blurted out, "You all should have told that girl, Angela, years ago that you were her father."

Ricky huffed, "Dr. Gates raised her as his. It made no sense to complicate thangs."

"So, it makes sense to complicate her life now?" Martha stated more than asked.

"Dis ain't me, ok? Last night, all y'all said dis was best. Da doctor told me he could be dere givin' her blood like he been givin' it ta her fo' years. But he did say it would better if I was dere while she was in labor. You heard him."

Martha stepped off the elevator first.

"I did hear him, and I am aware that this situation is not all your fault, but I think the girl is being put through a lot while she is pregnant."

She stopped in the hall, and the rubber soles of her sandals squeaked on the tile. Her head turned from left to right, and she realized she didn't know where Chester lived. I stepped by her taking the lead. When I turned the corner of the hallway, I saw three armed white men in front of Chester's door. I drew my pistol and Sonny lowered his ears; he was ready to bolt. Before I could make a move, Ricky's pistol was out, and he was advancing. "Muda fuckas, don't move. Drop yo weapons!"

They turned to face us, lowering their rifles but not dropping them. Sonny took off. "Stop!" I commanded. He stopped but didn't return to my side. He kept slowly approaching the armed white men.

"We are here on police business," the closest man claimed, slowly raising his rifle with his eyes on Sonny.

"With no radio and no badges," came from Mitchell. M&M had entered the hall through the exit door with their pistols also drawn. "They're not police, Mr. Price. We spotted them parking a van in the alley downstairs. We called the real police."

I saw the three armed men considering their odds. To help with their decision-making process, I quickly advanced with my pistol pointed at the speaker's head.

"You are outnumbered and outgunned. Don't die today."

They all slowly placed rifles and pistols on the stone-tiled floor. Ricky was shoulder to shoulder with me. "Dey wearin' SWAT shit."

Without me saying a word, M&M collected the weapons.

"On your knees," was my command. My son's door opened, and he stepped out of the condo.

I pointed to Chester and told Sonny, "Protect." Sonny walked to Chester's side.

"Call 911," Regina yelled. "Tell them armed men are trying to break into your apartment."

Chester quickly went back into the apartment and Sonny followed.

I told Regina, "Call Lee. Get him over here."

Regina and Martha hurried into the condo. It would have been a perfect ending to a bad situation if Harris and Lanham had been part of the three would-be assailants, but none of the white faces were familiar. But they were in SWAT attire.

"Y'all fucked up," Ricky said to the three.

They had gotten down on their knees and their hands were up. "You people are making a mistake interfering with official police business." The same man tried to bluff.

"Official police business my ass. Did Harris send you?" I asked.

"Who?" He truly sounded uninformed.

From behind us we heard, "Drop your weapons!" A group of uniformed police officers had turned the same hallway corner Ricky and I did. We all lowered our pistols.

M&M, Ricky, and I were cuffed along with the three intruders, and told to sit our "asses" on the floor. Ricky refused, "My knees won't let dat happen officer, ya will have ta call da paramedics ta help me get up off dat flo'."

A young Black policeman believed him and left the four of us cuffed and standing against the hallway wall.

I heard Regina, Martha, and Chester trying to leave the condo to check on us, but the police were not having it. They kept them inside.

"Damn, y'all too old to be in cuffs." It was Dixon. He and Lee walked by us laughing. They stopped at the three would-be assailants who were on their knees and cuffed.

Lee stood in front of the one who did all the talking. "James Hopkins, where did you get SWAT gear? Never mind, I know. You get one chance to answer this question. Listen closely, because your answer depends on the arresting charges: illegal possession of a firearm or armed home invasion. The choice is yours. Who gave you the job?"

Without hesitation he answered, "Rude Randy gave us the job."

"Targets?"

"Everybody in the place."

"When did he hire you?"

"I got the call around five this morning. We picked up the stuff at his place a couple of hours ago."

"And let me guess, you were supposed to leave these rifles."

"Yeah, those were his orders."

"Is that your van in the alley?"

"Yeah, we got that from Rude Randy too."

Dixon walked from the would-be assassin to Ricky. "A man with your associations must know Rude Randy." He uncuffed all four of us. "It's going to take us a minute to get these gentlemen processed and booked. By then Rude Randy may take flight or be clipped as a loose end." Dixon was not looking at either of us while he spoke. He was talking to the air.

Lee kicked over our pistols and said, "Sic him, boys," and turned away.

To me, Detective Dixon said, "You want to get to him before this mess goes public."

It became clear that Lee and Dixon were assisting more than hindering. More uniformed police came through the exit doors and from around the corner.

The police inside Chester's condo let Regina and Martha pass and they came directly to us.

Ricky told Martha, "The driver will meet you downstairs in five minutes. I'ma gonna text ya da address ta pick me and D. up in about an hour." He looked at Dixon and said, "I'ma need dey van keys." He nodded his head toward the cuffed white men

"I got those, Mr. Brown." Michael said and pulled a ring of keys from his back pocket and tossed them to Ricky. "I grabbed them when we went through the van."

Regina kissed me and said, "Be careful, David." I hugged her tight. While holding Regina in my arms, I gave M&M directions. "You two stay on my son, and good work."

*

I hadn't heard of Rude Randy, but Ricky had. "He's a fuckin' racist. He got rich makin' and sellin' crystal meth. Now he's inta erthang – he dank he da white Godfather, but he ain't. He just a young upstart. He a step-and-fetch-it boy fo' da real white gangsters in dis city. Dey throw him a bone er now and den."

Ricky had driven the van to a junkyard on Pershing Road. We pulled up to the junkyard gate and a skinny shaved-head kid came out of the shack. He looked at the van and not us and opened the gate. He went back into the shack.

"Ain't nobody here but dat kid, two yard hands, and Rude Randy sittin' in his office." Ricky opened the van door and got out. I followed him into the shack.

"Ricky Brown," the skinny bald kid said, backing up with his eyes bucked.

"We here to see Randy."

Ricky drew his pistol and spun the kid around, pushing him through a counter gate and past the counter. The kid landed in the only chair behind the counter. "Stay yo' ass right dere, and ya won't catch a bullet."

Rude Randy's office didn't have a door, so the bald, boyish-looking skinny kid with a black swastika tattooed on his forehead saw us coming. Ricky's pistol was out, and the would-be-crime boss managed to get his on his desk. He remained seated. His t-shirt had a sectioned snake across the chest with the words "Don't Tread on Me" above it.

"Ricky Brown. Good afternoon." He greeted Ricky and ignored me.

"Mr. Rude Randy, how da fuck is ya?"

Ricky didn't sit, so I didn't sit, but there were two chairs in front of the cluttered desk, and I really could have sat down because I was tired. The morning had moved nonstop.

"Three of yo' boys came to see my nephew. My blood."

Rude Randy's hands went up in surrender. "I didn't know. I got assigned a job with no name, just a place and orders."

Ricky thumbed the hammer back on his .45. "Who paid fo' da job?"

Rude Randy hesitated, but Ricky didn't; he shot him in the shoulder.

My attention went to the kid that was sitting behind the counter. He didn't seem to have any plans on moving, but I drew my pistol and placed my eyes on him anyway. The kid remained in the chair.

"Shit! Damn, Ricky Brown. The fat cop, don't kill me bro, please don't kill me. The fat cop, Lanham, gave me the job. Don't kill me, bro. I took the job to keep things copacetic between my business and the police. He keeps the cops off me, but I didn't know the job was your blood, Ricky Brown. I swear to God, I didn't know, bro."

"Stop callin' me bro. I'm not yo' fuckin' bro."

Holding his blood seeping shoulder, Rude Randy started humming and rocking to-and-fro in his desk chair.

"Don't kill me, Ricky Brown, please don't kill me, please."

Looking at the die-cast, cold-hearted, emotionless expression on Ricky's face, Rude Randy's begging for his life was appropriate. Ricky's nostrils were flaring with each breath, and he looked through Rude Randy. I was expecting another blast from the .45, but Ricky holstered his pistol.

There was a picture on the desk next to the phone. He picked it up. It was Rude Randy with an older woman. "You know White Helen?" Ricky held the framed picture in his hand still looking at it.

"What? Who?" Blood was seeping fast through Rude Randy's fingers. "That's me and my mom. I got to go to the hospital, man. Don't kill me, Ricky Brown."

"Yo mama? No shit." Ricky dropped the photo on the desk with a loud clank. He turned away from a begging-for-his-life Rude Randy, and we left the junkyard office, the junkyard shack, and the junkyard.

We were walking down Pershing Road with loud diesel fueled trucks passing us by. I heard Ricky saying, "His mama?"

Before I could ask Ricky what he was talking about, Martha's Lexus pulled up. Ricky climbed into the empty passenger seat, and I got into the back, causing Regina to scoot to the middle. I pulled the door closed against the noise of Pershing Road.

Inside the quieter Lexus, Ricky's worker said, "I didn't want to sit in front of the place."

"You did right," Ricky answered.

Martha asked, "Are ok, Ricky?"

"Erdang went good, baby." To me he said, "You know he's callin' Lanham right now."

"Yeah, and Lanham has to know we stopped his shooters. What was with the picture?"

"Dat was White Helen in dat picture. I didn't know she was his mama."

I almost laughed out loud, wondering if Rude Randy knew his mama got famous for the service she offered Black men? He was a known racist with a white hooker mama whose business was built on servicing Black men.

"Who is White Helen?" Regina asked.

"Nobody." Ricky and I answered too quickly.

"Ok... wow, don't bite a reporter's head off. Jesus. So, what else did you find out?" Regina asked me.

I turned my head to face her and said, "Lanham ordered those men to attack Chester."

She started blinking. "Wait, the police sergeant that was at the bank?"

I nodded my head yes, smiling. "One and the same."

"Wow. So that really connects the banker to the shooters?" She was sort of asking.

"Not really; it puts the banker in the pot with the shooter cops, but they are not stitched together, not yet," was my answer.

"Ok, so what happens next?" Martha asked us.

"Lanham and Harris have to be on alert now," Regina surmised.

"Which puts us on defense more than offense. They obviously see Chester as a threat." My son was protected, but I wanted to stop the threat.

"Will the attacks stop with the failed attempt?" Martha asked Ricky.

"Nope. Chester is a dreat because of what he doin'. We got ta let dem know dat dey ain't scarin' us inta stoppin'."

"You are talking about the police department," Regina stated.

Ricky shook his afro in the negative. "No, I ain't. It was da police dat came and arrested dose fuckas dat was goin' to kill Chester and Angela. We fixin' to kick some bullies asses, dat's who we fightin', some damn racist ass bullies."

My phone rang and Carol's name appeared. I answered.

"Your son is back on television. Live."

"What channel?"

"All of them, and M&M checked in, so I sent two more guards to assist. The way that boy is talking he's going to have the whole city after him." She hung up.

"Chester is on television," I told the other passengers.

"What?" All but the driver asked simultaneously.

"Y'all heard me." I was the only one smiling.

Regina said, "My place is closer, and I record all the news broadcasts. Let go there." She told the driver, "1822 South Clark Street."

The driver looked to Ricky, who nodded his head yes.

*

I never thought of Regina's living room as small, but with four adults in it, I realized she didn't furnish it with company in mind. There were two bar stools at the counter that separated the kitchen, a wicker rocker, and a love seat. Ricky sat in the love seat, and Regina sat in the rocker. She cut on the small flatscreen that sat on an end table next to a pole lamp with no shade. Martha and I sat on the stools at the counter. It didn't take Regina three seconds to find Chester.

"My friend, Wilson Norton, the activist who was shot down by Officer Redding of the Chicago Police Department, believed protesting makes a difference. He believed only the squeaky wheel got the oil. He believed when people were quiet, they got rolled over by adversaries. In my heart, I am certain he was killed for that belief. He was killed because he would not be quiet about police shootings. He was killed because he would not be silent about Grant Federal Savings exploiting Black and LatinX families trying to buy homes.

"He was killed because he wanted a fair and equitable life for all people. The Chicago police arrested three armed assailants at my door this afternoon. Three! Inside my home were me and my pregnant girlfriend. Why were they here? Why were three men at my door armed with rifles and dressed in SWAT attire? Why?

"I suggest we ask Chicago police officers Alfred Harris and Jeffery Lanham, and I think we should ask Grant Federal Savings Vice President Theodore Drayman." My son paused and looked into the cameras.

A reporter asked, "Why would these men be informed about armed intruders at your door?"

"Because they have information relating to Wilson Norton's shooting as well."

"Are you saying the events are connected?"

"Of course."

"And what proof do you have?"

"That information is forthcoming, but if you want to get the scoop, see officers Lanham or Harris or Theodore Drayman at Grant Federal Savings. They have all the answers you seek."

Chester smiled, nodded his head and then turned his back on the reporters. He walked through the revolving glass doors of his condominium building, ending the press conference.

"All righty then, it appears our son has a plan of his own." Regina clicked off her small television.

Chester's plan was closely related to my original plan. He was using the media to attack his foes.

"Da boy is smart, but we still gotta push ahead wid what we doin'. Deses fuckas ain't goin' stop because people heard dey names. Dese cops is use to havin' dey way. Dey need a reason ta stop. Dey need some pain in dey lives."

Regina argued, "I disagree. Chester has done enough. No way those policemen or the banking executive will act against him now. The whole city is watching him."

Martha asked, "Does he really have information linking those men to his friend's shooting?"

I answered, "No. He is bluffing, which is why Ricky is right. The threat is still present, and we have to eliminate it before it tries to strike again. Those men at Chester's door were the threat striking. Lanham wasn't there, Harris wasn't there, and Drayman wasn't there, but they threw the blow. It was their attempt. People saying their names means nothing to powerful men like them. They have to fear us, see us an equal threat."

Ricky rose from the loveseat without a huff. He was a six three, four-hundred-pound man in gangster mode. "I'ma pick ya up 'bout 5:30 for our six o'clock wid Lanham."

"Ok. Where is the meet?"

"Bar Louie's on Chicago Avenue." Ricky answered.

I liked the place. It was where I had my first black and tan ale.

"Are we still going to talk to Angela?" Martha asked him.

"Nope, not today, baby, but we will."

After walking Ricky and Martha to Regina's front door, I joined Regina at the kitchen counter. I looked down at my gold Presidential Rolex, a gift from another case, and realized I had less than four hours before the meeting.

She asked me, "You really think I'm wrong about the media coverage being enough?"

I sat on the stool next to her. "Yeah, I do. These men have been intoxicated with privilege; the media is only one of their tools. Chester's interview will disappear in half a day, and people will forget their names were ever mentioned. Tell me this - has there been a public protest about Lanham being named the head of SWAT after shooting down a Black man? No, because people forget names, and those in power control that forgetfulness."

Regina's cellphone vibrated on the counter.

She picked it and answered, "Hey Chester. Yes, of course. I should expect her now? Ok, that will be fine. Love you."

To me she said, "He gave Angela's cousin, Alice, the girl from the bank, my address. She is on way her over here."

"Why?"

"He didn't say. He was on the other line with her."

The door chime rang, and Regina quickly rose to answer it. I got up from the stool and took the rocker. If I had let my eyes close, I could have napped despite everything that was going on.

Alice entered the living area following behind Regina. She and Regina took the stools at the counter. She was barely seated when she began, "The lady from Human Resources and two security guards came in and walked

Mr. Drayman out of the bank. They wouldn't let him take his briefcase or anything, but he did take his phone. He looked like he wanted to tell his secretary to do something, but he didn't.

"He was silent while they walked him out. And get this, as soon as the elevator doors closed, Ms. Chambers, his secretary stood and clapped her hands and said, "Praise Jesus, he was the worst man I ever worked for." Then she went down a list of all the things he did wrong. She expected him to get fired months ago.

"She ordered us sandwiches and told me not worry about my internship because interns were always reassigned after management changes. She gave me the rest of the day off and told me to report to her in the morning. They fired him, and I figured you would want to know."

I was shocked and leaned forward in the rocker.

Regina nodded her head and said, "He is going to be the scapegoat. Those above him are aware of the story breaking, and Chester mentioning of his name was probably the straw that broke the camel's back. They are going to blame the loan program on Drayman. I expect a statement in the morning."

Still sitting, Alice said, "I'm just happy I get to keep the internship. Do you think the bank executives will help the people that lost their homes and got the bad loans?"

Regina shook her head to the negative but said, "They will have to do something. I and others are not going to let it rest. Something will happen."

Alice stood up. "Good, then maybe their friend's death won't be completely in vain. I am going to miss seeing him on the television, Wilson Norton, but your son and my cousin seem to be keeping things going. Ok then..." She exhaled. "I just wanted to tell you all about Drayman being fired. I'm going home. Ms. Chambers still wants the sales reports in the morning." Alice waved goodbye to me and followed Regina to the front door.

When Regina returned, she sat in my lap.

"Do you think she's right?"

"About?"

"People thinking of Chester as they did Wilson Norton?"

"Yep, I believe so. If he keeps protesting, he will become the squeaky wheel, and all eyes will be on him."

"I'm not sure that is a good thing."

"Good thing or bad thing - it is his thing," and I kissed my baby's mama.

Chapter Twelve

When I woke up, Regina was sitting next to me in the bed with her laptop in her lap.

"White Helen is a well-known madam with a brothel in prestigious Beverly. It appears she rose to fame after her pimp disappeared, and she began managing his prostitutes herself. Did you know that?"

Did I know that? Of course, I knew that. I was an intimate part of her rise, but what I said was "Seems like I remember hearing something like that."

"Well, there is this website that posts pictures of current and older Chicago hustlers; and look here, there are several pictures of you, her, and Ricky Brown. Imagine that."

I knew about the damn website and the posted pictures. The pictures were from a player's ball, a fashion show, and a picnic.

"Me? Let me see. I knew her and Ricky was friends, but pictures of me? Are you sure?"

Looking at the photos there was no denying it was me, so I tried to act surprised and innocent.

"Oh man, don't I look young?"

"You do, and so does Ricky and the white woman. The three of you could be mistaken for high school friends if not for the relaxed hair, the tailor-made clothes, the jewelry, and the furs. Who was White Helen to you?"

I really didn't want to answer that question.

*

Ricky started going to see White Helen regularly, sometimes twice a day, and at the very least every other day. He told me, "She only charge me when Steady Freddy is dere. And get dis, she had me fuck two of da other girls, so he wouldn't guess we had a thang goin'."

"A thing? You got a thing going on with a hooker?"

"Naw, not really. We just be chillin'." He looked at me sideways as he turned corner. The long-handled shovels clanked together in the back of his Eldorado.

"What's up anyway? What couldn't wait until tomorrow?"

I'd just moved into my first apartment, and it was my second night there, and it was my first time cooking myself a meal in my own place: fried catfish and spaghetti. I was getting my face greasy when Ricky came banging on my door a little after midnight.

"Like I told, ya. I got a situation. We almost dere."

The "there" he was talking about was the garage of an abandoned house. Nothing good ever happened in one of those, and I knew it. I was tempted to stay in the Cadillac after Ricky parked it between the high bushes in the backyard, but I didn't.

Inside the garage, White Helen was sitting in chair with a long yellow candle in her hand. Next to her chair were four bags of concrete mix and two tall black plastic buckets. A pickax was in the middle of the floor next to a hole busted into the concrete down to the dirt, and a four-foot-high pile of dirt was next to the hole. Ricky handed me one of the shovels he'd carried into the garage.

In the chair behind the hole was a duct tape-gagged Steady Freddy. I could see his wide-open eyes in the dim candlelight.

"What? You finna kill Steady Freddy?" I whispered to Ricky.

"Yeah, I dank so." He walked to the hole and stuck the shovel into the dirt.

I was trying to figure out if was I there to help dig the hole or talk him out of it.

White Helen stood from her chair and walked over to Steady Freddy. "If we don't kill him, he will kill us. I swear to God he will."

The candlelight was creeping me out, and the whole situation looked way too dastardly.

White Helen kept talking. "He kills people that move him against him. I saw him beat a girl to death. He killed his own father. He will kill us... me. He will kill me."

She was looking down at him, but he was looking at us. Through the candlelight, I saw the fear in his eyes. I looked away from Steady Freddy to Ricky.

"What happened?" I asked.

But he didn't answer me; instead, he screamed, "No!"

When I looked back to Steady Freddy, I saw White Helen slicing Steady's throat open with a straight razor. I didn't move and Ricky didn't move. She cut him clean and deep. The blood poured, and Steady Freddy's head dropped with his eyes still open. The fear was gone. His eyes were just open.

White Helen closed the black-handled razor with a flick of her wrist while still holding the candle in her other hand. "Finish the hole, and let's get him in it," she said to Ricky and me.

Leaving was the smart thing to do, but I didn't leave. We dug while White Helen mixed the concrete. When the hole reached the city sewer pipe, we stopped. We climbed out the hole covered in sweat. I followed Ricky over to the chair that held Steady Freddy. Ricky put his arms under Steady Freddy's armpits, and I grabbed his knees. The body made a thud when it hit the sewer pipe. We filled the hole with the dirt and busted concrete rocks. We patted the mound of dirt and rocks as flat as we could with the shovels. White Helen poured the wet sandy concrete. She used a Marvin Gay album cover to spread the concrete smooth.

She stuffed the concrete bags and the album cover into a bucket and told us, "We have to take the buckets and stuff with us. Drop them two or three alleys down."

I wanted to go home, but Ricky didn't drive me back to my new apartment. We went to what used to be Steady Freddy's place across the street from the park. White Helen sent two Black girls into the room with me, and that night became one of the freakiest sexual memories of my life.

The next morning, when I woke up, White Helen was in the bed with me. All while we were fucking, she clung to me like another layer of skin. She wouldn't let me withdraw from her body even after I ejaculated; she kept me inside of her until I got hard again. She did that two times, and she kept telling me, "We are linked in deed, and in body. We are family, D."

That afternoon, she gave me three of Steady Freddy's gold chains and one of his diamond rings. The next day, I arranged the sale of his Corvette, and my share was thirty-five hundred dollars. Ricky Brown got the rest of Steady Freddy's jewelry, and White Helen introduced him to the sex trade. She chose him.

*

Regina interrupted my memories with "D., I asked you who or what was White Helen to you?"

I kept my gaze on her laptop screen.

"I told you, she was more Ricky's friend than mine. She was with him in those pictures. I was the third wheel. I barely knew her."

Regina moved her head to the negative and said, "Ok, barely knew her, she's almost butt naked sitting on your lap in this picture."

"That's just how she dressed; she was always half naked. She was just an associate."

"Ok, if you say so."

"I say so."

I turned away from Regina and her laptop, fluffed my pillow, and dozed back off.

*

Ricky picked me up in Martha's Lexus, and he was driving it himself. I expected it to be just me and him. I had two .9mms and an extra clip for each. He u-turned on

Clark Street and headed north. I was thinking, well hoping, the guns would only be for show. I didn't anticipate the life-or-death situation that erupted.

"You and Gina still gettin' married again, right?" Ricky snickered. "You ain't never stopped lovin' her. You probably still dank she da finest woman in da world, don't cha?"

"I do." I started grinning because it was true; Regina was the finest woman in the world. "And yeah, we doing it at City Hall then going to Barbados, just me and her."

Muddy Waters' Mannish Boy was playing on Lexus' sound system. My head couldn't help but rock to Muddy's beat.

I saw Ricky's eyebrows raise.

"Ok den, Martha thought y'all was usin' our place."

My head was still rocking; I loved Muddy.

"Regina wants it small and over as soon as possible."

"She scared ya gonna get cold feet?"

"Nope, not at all. She knows I ain't going nowhere."

"I'm happy fo' ya, D. If ya happy, I'm happy."

There was a silver Escalade pulling out of park as we pulled up to Bar Louie's, and Ricky grabbed the spot.

When we walked in the bar, it was almost empty, which was never the case. The place was always busy and packed with customers. I immediately saw Harris, the new head of SWAT, sitting at the bar with a neat shot in front of him. He was not dressed in SWAT gear. He had on a sky-blue New Balance running suit with white New Balance track shoes, and he was built like a runner.

He only glanced at us as if we were insignificant. But for me, the situation got a lot tenser seeing his blue-eyed ass sitting at the bar. What I thought and speculated became real with Harris being present. The connection between the rogue officers was in front of me, and they obviously did not care if I knew they were associated.

A tall LatinX bartender was standing behind the bar, he nodded to a table, and the guy sitting at the table was Lanham. Ricky and I stepped to the table. Lanham had a huge order of chicken wings in front of him, and there were three armed uniformed SWAT officers about four paces away from the him and his table. I smelled garlic coming from the wings. Lanham was still in a sergeant's white uniform shirt. He extended his hand to the two empty chairs. We sat. One of the SWAT officers walked past us to the front of the restaurant bar, blocking the entrance.

Lanham, who also looked at us as if we were insignificant irritants, said, "This is how things will proceed. David Price, you will get your son to cease and desist with the police protest. If that happens, he won't meet the same fate as Wilson Norton."

He spoke as if he had called the meeting, and he was blatantly threating my son's life.

"He and his group got Drayman fired, Pinker is dead, and you killed Redding. Hell... let's call it done and end it. Stop the fucking protest!"

He looked from me to Ricky, then back at me. He grabbed a wing from the bowl and stripped it of its flesh and tossed the naked bone onto an empty paper plate next to his platter of wings.

Ricky shook his big head to the negative and said, "No, dis how dings will go. I'm holdin' 50k worth of yo' markers and unless yo fat ass can pay me right now... you gonna fo'get my nephew is alive. I don't give a fuck what he is protestin,' you stay da fuck away from him."

Lanham huffs. "I'm a police officer. You can shove those markers up your goddamn ass. I know who and what you are, Ricky Brown. You don't scare me."

Ricky was up from the chair in a breath upending the table and scattering the platter of chicken wings across the floor. His pistol was out and in Lanham's mouth. I stood and drew both of my pistols; one was pointing at the two SWAT officers a few steps away, and my other pistol was moving between Harris and the SWAT officer at the door, and that was not an easy aiming situation; both seemed anxious to move.

Ricky thumbed the hammer back of his .45, "Mudafucka you owe me fifty large. I don't give a fuck 'bout you bein' da police."

The SWAT officer by the door moved. I released a round that landed in the wooden floorboard six inches in front of him; he stopped. Harris remained seated at the bar, and the bartender stood behind the bar with his hands up.

"I was gonna give ya a week, but I want to get paid today, bitch! Or ya a dead fuckin' police officer."

Ricky built his reputation on being irrational and doing the unexpected. Blowing a hole in Lanham's head was the unexpected. I thought the fat cop was dead. Matter of fact, I doubted that me, Ricky, Lanham, or Harris was going to make out of the bar alive. The shootout was going to be bloody, but what happened next stunned me.

Regina pushed her way through the front door of Bar Louie's with a cameraman. She approached the bar asking, "Commander Harris, what are your comments on Grant Banking executive Theodore Drayman naming you and Officer Lanham in the Wilson Norton shooting?"

Harris instantly stood from the bar stool. "What the hell are you talking about? Get that camera out of here, and you get out of my face!" He made the mistake of shoving Regina back, causing her to tumble backwards, almost falling. I moved to him without thought. Two pistol butt blows to each temple sent Harris to his knees.

Regina and her cameraman changed focus and stepped to a standing Lanham. Ricky holstered his pistol, which Regina and her cameraman ignored. SWAT officers came to Harris' aide. He was attempting to stand, but kept dropping to his knees. I was the closest to him, but I offered no assistance and holstered my weapons.

Regina had her mic in Lanham's face. "Twenty minutes ago, Theodore Drayman admitted to having a conversation where the three of you agreed that Chicago would be a better city without Wilson Norton. Drayman stated that during this conversation it was agreed that a SWAT raid would solve the problem."

Lanham dusted off his white uniform shirt without answering.

"Were you there the night Wilson Norton was killed? Did you have that conversation with Theodore Drayman?"

Lanham kept wiping chicken wing crumbs from his clothes. All three SWAT officers were helping Harris stand. The blows to the temples had wrecked his equilibrium.

Lanham, who was still ignoring Regina, told me, "You are under arrest for assaulting a police officer." He placed his hand on my shoulder and was attempting to turn me around.

"Why aren't you arresting the man that just shoved a pistol down your throat?" I asked him.

Regina asked, "What?"

"This doesn't concern you, Miss. Please step back," Lanham ordered.

Since I was not offering any resistance, he almost had the cuffs on me when another astonishing event occurred. Detectives Frost and Beverly entered the bar with about six uniformed officers. The three SWAT officers had succeeded in steadying Harris although on wobbly legs.

Detective Frost approached me, Regina, and Lanham. He took the cuffs from Lanham's hands and pulled his own cuffs out from beneath his suit jacket.

"Richard Lanham, you are under arrest for conspiracy to comment murder." Frost spun Lanham around and cuffed his fat ass.

Beverly was repeating the same charges to Harris and cuffing him despite his poor gait. The uniformed officers moved to and cuffed the other SWAT officers. I had never seen police arresting police in my life, and by the large grin that crossed Ricky's face, I assumed it was a first for him too. The police hauled the arrested out of the bar to waiting Chicago Police Department SUVs. We stood inside the bar looking out the large bar window. Detectives Lee and Dixon entered the bar.

"You didn't see that coming, did you, security guard?" Dixon asked me. He had walked to the window and was standing between me and Ricky.

I didn't see it coming, so I answered, "Nope, not at all," still looking out at the police presence. How could I have seen it coming? I barely understood what had happened.

Detective Lee beelined to the bar and sat on a stool. He gave the bartender a hand signal, and the tall man started frosting a mug. "Yeah, it all started with the thugs we arrested at your son's apartment. The leader, James Hopkins, rolled over repeatedly on Rude Randy.

"We went to see Rude Randy at the hospital. He was suffering from a gunshot wound to the shoulder. He said he accidently shot himself cleaning a pistol." Lee moved his head to look over at Ricky who stood silent looking out the window. "Anyway," Lee turned back to the bartender, "once I informed Rude Randy of the charges he was actually facing relating to the stolen SWAT uniforms and the stolen rifles from police lockup, and the contracting of assassins, he didn't hesitate in telling us who actually paid him, and that turned out to be the key." He paused, looked over at us and smiled. He took several big gulps from his frosted mug before he continued.

"Police work is multilayered. Most civilians like yourselves don't understand that. What we do is far deeper than what the public sees." He took another gulp of the ale. It looked like Guinness. "Rude Randy told us a banker actually paid to hire the shooters at your son's place. I got him on tape saying it. When we went to see the banker, and played the tape, he sang his ass off."

The police presence was gone from the front of Bar Louie's, so we all walked from the window to the bar and sat on the stools with Lee. "We" included Regina, her cameraman, Ricky, me, and Dixon. Regina and her cameraman sat on one side of Lee and Dixon, and Ricky and I sat on the other.

Lee continued with, "But the shocker was Rude Randy sending us to Helen Swift. I didn't believe what he told us."

Dixon nodded his head at Lee's frosted mug, and the bartender went to work on another. Dixon chuckled and said, "Nobody would have believed it. The brainiacs were at Helen Swift's whorehouse sitting in her smoking room putting the fucked-up plans together. When Rude Randy told me that, I thought he was bullshitting. Until he said, 'my mama got tapes of us talking.'

"It appears they were watching Wilson Norton's protests on television when they realized they had a common enemy. Norton's televised protest brought them together."

I was confused, so I asked, "Wait, what are you saying? Norton's protest?"

Dixon turned his face to me and grinned. "Yeah."

The bartender slid Dixon's beer down the bar to him.

Regina asked Dixon, "Are you saying that Lanham, Harris, Pinker, Redding, and the banker Drayman all used this Helen Swift's services?"

Lee answered, shaking his head in the affirmative. "Yes, at different times at first, but it appears once they started planning, they met there regularly. When we went to see Helen Swift, because of what Rude Randy said about her having tapes, we didn't even have to tell her why we were there. She handed us video tapes of the conversations at the front door. Do you hear me? We didn't even ask her for them. We rang the doorbell; she opened the door and handed us the tapes."

Ricky said, "She tapes erdang dat happens in dat place, includin' da fuckin'."

I saw concerned looks appear on every man's face at the bar, including Dixon and Lee.

Ricky told the bartender, "Give me a orda of dem chicken wings wid hot sauce."

Regina's cameraman told her, "Done. It's sent. They are going to play the interview on the website while they are announcing the arrest. We are the only source in the city with the story. It is breaking news, baby!" They gave each other a high-five.

There were no other media present at the arrest. I saw Lee and Regina sharing a grin. The cameraman said, "Drinks on me!"

I leaned to Ricky and asked him, "Can you drop me at Chester's?" I wanted to see my son, to see for myself that he was ok, because the threat did not feel gone. Danger was still about. I felt it.

"Yeah, as soon as dude brings me my wings we gone."

Regina was talking into her phone and typing on her iPad. I stood from the barstool and went to her. I whispered into her available ear, "Going to see Chester. Meet you at my place tonight." I kissed her on the cheek and avoided looking at Lee. She nodded her head in the affirmative and kept talking and typing. Ricky was standing at the bar and paying the bartender for the chicken wings.

The first rounds shattered the bar's large plate glass front window. I turned and dropped down to the wooden floor, and I saw four bald white men firing automatic rifles into Bar Louie's. Almost everyone sitting at the bar made it to the floor. Ricky, me, Dixon, and Lee fired our pistols from the floor. I put two rounds in the bald head on the far left. I don't know who shot who after I fired, but all four were dropped. When we stood, I saw the cameraman slumped over the bar; he had been shot in the back of his head.

When Regina saw his corpse, she began screaming nonstop. Before I could get to her, Lee pulled her into his arms, and she wept in his embrace. I went outside with my pistol still in my hand. All the shooters were dead. They had all been shot in the head. Ricky and Dixon came out with me.

I wanted to shoot all the shooters again. I wanted to empty my clip into their skulls.

"Mudafuckas," Ricky said kicking the shooter closest to him in the head.

Dixon gave me another surprise when he asked Ricky, "Do you need to leave?"

Ricky answered, "Nope, I got a concealed carry permit. Dis was legal." My fat friend grinned at the detective.

*

It didn't take fifteen minutes for the police presence to blanket Bar Louie's, again. The practical thing for the buzzing police presence to consider was that all the shooters were dead which meant there was no one to ask what they were doing there. No one to ask who sent them and why. However, the police presence was more concerned with collecting shells and confiscating weapons.

I stood outside the bar and answered about ten dumbass questions and turned over one of my .9mms. I didn't go back into the bar because I didn't want see

Regina or Lee. Him comforting her had pissed me off. Fuck her dead cameraman; Lee's arms should not have been around her. I knew the thought was selfish and immature, but it was my feeling, and I held on to it.

Despite getting shot at, Ricky had his order of chicken wings in hand. "You still ridin' wid me?"

"Yep."

"Let's roll."

An officer stopped traffic for us, and Ricky pulled Martha's Lexus onto Chicago Avenue. The streetlights, headlights, and shop lights provided the illumination of the night. Looking up at the dark blue sky, I couldn't see a star, but the moon was there.

"Martha called. She wants to go over Chester's wid us. You cool wid dat?"

"No problem."

"What da fuck was dat about? Who was dey tryin' to kill?"

"I don't know, man. But they knocked on the wrong door that's for damn sure; not one was left alive."

"Maybe dey was afda Regina."

His words made me sit up straight.

"What makes you say that?"

"Who else was important? She was puttin' out da story."

"You think them shooting us up like that was about her story? The people who the story is about got arrested. I don't think they were there for Regina. Nothing is making any sense."

I didn't want to talk; I wanted to think.

Chapter Thirteen

When Ricky pulled up to his house, I got out of the Lexus, giving Martha the front passenger seat. Her hair was in rollers, and she had a yellow scarf covering them. One of Ricky's workers held the SUV door open for her. I climbed into the backseat and closed my own door; the worker closed Martha's door, and Ricky pulled off. I could see the stars in the night sky over the lake.

My phone rang; it was Regina. Martha greeted Ricky and me, and I returned her greeting, but my "hello" didn't sound as cheerful and warm as hers.

I answered Regina's call and heard her saying, "I will meet you over at Chester's – in a cab on my way now."

"Ok, we are just leaving Ricky's see you there." I quickly hung up because part of me wanted to ask why Lee wasn't dropping her off. Hearing her voice brought the anger front and center in my mind. I didn't want to sound as jealous and as insecure as I felt.

"I saw the arrest on the news, so things are working themselves out, right? Chester and Angela are out of danger, right?" Martha asked Ricky and me.

I wanted to tell her yes, but the certainty that was needed to say the word wasn't present. I sensed danger lurking, and I guessed Ricky had not told her about us getting shot at.

"Almost, baby. Dere is just a few loose ends, but we are goin' to talk to Angela tonight, ok?"

Martha did not respond. She looked out the passenger window to the dark lake. I had forgotten Ricky was to tell Angela he was her father. All of that had eased from my mind. It wasn't just my son that was in danger: the mother of my grandchild and my grandchild were in danger as well.

Ricky cut Muddy Waters back on, and I took advantage of the playing music and checked the clip in my remaining .9mm. I had only surrendered one to the police. The clip was full, and I had three more in my holster. I put my pistol back in place, and my mind went back to Regina and Lee sharing a grin at the bar. My thinking was tripping, and I knew it. I needed to talk.

"Ricky, remember the first time we saw Muddy Waters on stage?"

"Yeah, we was kids, but we dought we was grown – down on Navy Pier. Yeah, I remember."

A big grin opened his pudgy face, and I started grinning too.

"It was a good time."

"A damn good time, first time I drank moonshine."

Our grins turned to chuckles with the memory.

"I remember; the little old fella had a couple of mason jars in his cooler. Sweet Jesus, it was a miracle we made it home."

"Yeah, but he tried to tell us; whad he say – a lil sip a do ya. And I don't dank ya can call sleepin' in da backyard rollin' around in our own piss and puke makin' it home. Ya daddy came out wid da hose and washed us down in da grass. Jesus, we was a mess sho' nuff. Da next afternoon, we both swore ta da good Lord we was dro drankin', and we was fo' about five days."

"Yeah, but ten years passed before I tried moonshine again." Ricky had cut through the park, so the ride to Chester's was quick.

I told him, "I got the parking valet."

"Cool."

Suddenly, Ricky stopped getting out of the SUV. He turned his big head to face me. "Dere is dis dang bouncin' around in my head. I need ya ta find out were dey took Rude Randy."

I pulled out my phone and pushed 'asshole.'

"What's up, Price?" Lee queried.

"What hospital is Rude Randy in?"

"U of C. Why?"

I hung up without answering him.

"The hospital around the corner. What's up?"

"Dis shit ain't over."

"Ricky?" Martha asked.

He turned around to face her. "Almost, baby, we will be right back." He looked back at me. "I don't know how we missed it, D. Dem shooters was baldheaded."

"Rude Randy."

"Naw ya brain workin'."

I was thinking, but it wasn't clear. Why would a low-level, wannabe crime boss have people shoot at us? I asked Ricky, "Revenge, because you shot him in the shoulder?"

"Don't have a fuckin' clue, but it was him. I know it."
He burned rubber pulling from the entryway of Chester's
condominium. Ricky was driving the Lexus so hard the
hospital parking attendant hopped back up on the curve
when we pulled in. I didn't understand the rush or why
Rude Randy was the target, but I followed along.

Ricky handed the valet a fifty and asked, "Gunshot
wound to the shoulder with a cop outside, what floor?"

"Probably 3 West." The valet took the fifty, tore a
ticket and gave the numbered end to Ricky. Still hurrying,
Ricky pushed through the hospital's revolving doors and
walked to the closest bank of elevators. Martha and I were
in the whirlwind of his mass.

We exited the elevator on 3W. Ricky walked by the
nurses' station with us in tow. There was a policeman
standing outside one room, and he zoomed to that room
only to be stopped by the officer's, "No visitors."

A female voice told the guard to, "Let him in, please."

Ricky almost pushed the policeman aside.

When Martha and I got to the room, the officer offered
no resistance, so we entered following Ricky.

Rude Randy was sitting up in the bed holding a white
styrofoam cup with a straw. He was sipping though the
straw, but my attention went to what he was missing. His
left arm was gone.

"Damn, Ricky Brown, you're still alive." Rude Randy
stated.

"What did you just say, Randy?" The woman in the
bedside chair asked. Her back was to us.

"I asked that nigger was he still alive. What else can he do to me, Ma? Fuck him."

The Rude Rudy in the hospital bed was different than Rude Randy in the junkyard shack. The one in the hospital bed did not appear afraid of Ricky Brown... at all.

"He fucked up the biggest deal of my life, Ma. The biggest! And he took my arm. These niggers are supposed to be dead. Dead!" He screamed trying to rise, but the pain immediately stopped him. He whimpered and slumped back onto the stacked pillows that braced his back. "Fucking niggers."

The woman in the chair stood and turned around to face us. She was wearing form-fitting blue jeans and a pink silk blouse the was unbuttoned to just above her navel. She had on pink gym shoes with no socks, and I doubted that she wore any type of undergarments. Panties and bras were seldom part of White Helen's attire.

"My apologies, Ricky Brown. My son is full of pain medicine."

They embraced. While hugging Ricky, she glanced over to me and smiled. She looked down at my hand. I still wore the ring. It was two-carat pinky ring– of course I still wore it.

"Hey D."

"Hey Helen."

Rude Randy started kicking his feet in the bed.

"Stop it, Ma! Don't touch that nigger! What the hell are you doing?"

Ignoring Rude Randy's protest, White Helen asked our group, "Shall we step out and talk?"

It was Martha who answered, "Yes."

As we turned and proceeded toward the doorway we heard, "Ma, come back! Don't leave this room with those niggers! Come back here!"

White Helen didn't stop walking, and once we were in the hospital hall, she led us to a small family consultation room.

Martha and White Helen sat at a small faux wood table. I grabbed the blue and gray striped armchair, and Ricky took the loveseat with same pattern.

White Helen adjusted in her chair and exhaled. "My son is a racist pig. He has always been a vile creature. He was raised downstate by my racist rapist father who is actually... my son's father." She dropped the painful fact on us without pausing. "My son is not right in the head... he has never been right in the head. As a child, he ate bugs, particularly cockroaches. My ignorant hateful father died seven years ago, and the boy came up here to live with me."

There was no grief in her words. "The bastard that was my father, taught Randy how to make crystal meth, and this city embraced my hateful son due to his meth cooking skill, and that inclusion allotted him a little power. He found people who shared my father's racist beliefs, and he has prospered with them.

"The banker, Drayman, filled his head with promises of chasing Blacks and Hispanics out of their homes. That was the big deal he was crying about losing. Supposedly, all across the country, white people who believed what he believed were going to be empowered to evict Black and Hispanic families from their homes.

"When Drayman was fired, Randy saw that as the end of the world - add that to the doctor taking his arm after you shot him, and you have my deranged son trying to kill you." Her words were targeting Ricky, but her black eyes went from person to person in the small room, and they settled with Martha.

She adjusted herself in the chair as she spoke, and I found myself wanting her open blouse to open just a bit more, but it didn't.

"I didn't know Rude Randy was ya son." Ricky said, leaning forward in the loveseat.

"No one I associate with does. However, Randy's associates and his underlings did. Neither Drayman nor Harris was aware of our family connection. The fat one, Lanham may have known.

"I have relocation plans to Tampa, and that planning has been occupying my thoughts. The happenings of this city have been minimal in my thinking. Police shootings and such are not my focus. Harris' marriage proposal along with your request, Ricky, broke through my... stupor – if you will.

"And after Ricky told me that was your son on television, I surrendered the tapes to the detectives, hoping to end it all. We are still family after all."

Martha asked, "What tapes are you speaking of, and why would you have them?"

White Helen smiled, and age hadn't diminished her attraction. "The tapes were made in my gentlemen's smoking room, and without taking too much credit, it was the tapes that lead to Drayman's, Lanham's, Harris', and even my dumbass son's arrest."

Martha cocked her yellow-scarfed head and asked, "Your gentlemen's smoking room?" She was cutting around the edges of White Helen's words, and not knowing how much she knew about White Helen, things got tense for me in the small room.

"It's a den really. A place for customers to relax and have a good smoke and a strong drink. Randy worked as the bartender in the room when he first arrived. That was how he got familiar with Drayman and the police officers."

"Customers?" Martha queried.

White Helen looked to Ricky and me without answering Martha.

"She is a madam, Martha," was the answer I gave.

"Oh… I understand, and your son was a worker at your establishment?" Martha untied and retied her scarf under her chin. She looked over at Ricky, then back to White Helen.

White Helen nodded yes. "For a while, but once he made associations he got started in business on his own. He continued to bring the house business and to use the provided services. I am certain my establishment helped him to elevate his status.

"He made good connections. My clientele includes patrolman, gang leaders, alderman, bankers, bank robbers, senators, cooks - men from all walks of life use the services I provide." White Helen did not look at me or Ricky; her gaze stayed with Martha.

Martha pushed her chair back a bit from the table, creating more distance between herself and White Helen. "I can imagine, and the tapes helped how?"

Before White Helen could answer, a frustrated Indian nurse quickly entered the small family room. "I am sorry, Ms. Swift, but your son is demanding to see you. Please, could you come calm him down before he opens his wound?"

*

At Chester's building, the parking valet handed me a ticket, and I handed him a twenty because I knew I wasn't riding back with Ricky. I gave Ricky the paid ticket, and the three us walked through the glass doors. When we got to the elevator, the doors opened, and Sonny and Angela were getting off. My dog looked at me and smiled and wagged his tail. We stepped back, letting them off the elevator.

"I was taking him for a short walk, Mr. Price. I need some air, and he does too." Chester must have given Sonny the friend command for Angela.

Martha asked Angela, "Do you mind if we walk with you, Mr. Brown and I?"

"Oh no, not all." Looking up at me through her thick black glasses, Angela said, "Mrs. Price is upstairs, and she told us everything. We are so glad it is over." Again, she gave me a quick awkward hug. "Thank you for keeping us safe, Mr. Price. And she told us about you guys getting married again. I think that is so wonderful."

I hugged her back and said, "You are family now, and we keep ours safe." I did not comment on the wedding news; I only smiled at her and nodded my head. Sonny looked up at me, so I gave him the hand gesture to continue, and the four of them went down the driveway while I pushed through the revolving doors. The fatherhood conversation was between the Browns and Gates.

Chester opened his apartment door with a big grin on his face. "Mom updated us. The threat is over, and you guys are jumping the broom!" He hugged me and I hugged him back.

Regina was sitting on the couch with her green eyes sparkling, and her whole face was opened in a smile. She truly looked happy, and there was no way I was going to interject anything negative into the mood of the room. I released a smile of my own and held on tight to my son.

While hugging him, I asked, "And ain't that something about Ricky being the other granddaddy?"

My son stepped back from the embrace. "What?" He was still smiling. "I'm not sure what you are talking about, Dad?"

Regina stood up from the couch and said, "Ricky Brown is Angela's biological father."

My son started laughing. "What?" He shook his head no. "Oh, that can't be right. Dr. Gates is the clingiest, possessive, and the most overprotective father I have ever known. God, he involves himself in every aspect of Angela's life. You must be mistaken, Mom."

My son sat on the couch and Regina returned to sitting. I sat in a plastic chair at the small kitchen table.

"There is no mistake. Ricky and Martha are telling her now," I said.

My son was smiling, but still shaking his head no. "I mean it doesn't make me a difference, but the news will probably shake Angela up a bit; she loves Dr. Gates." He stopped smiling and said, "But, you know, she did ask me a lot of questions about Ricky last night, and I told her what I knew." My son paused and cast his eyes over to me. "Thinking about, I might be more surprised than her."

Regina queried, "What kind of stuff did she ask you?"

"You know, the gangster stuff, all of that. I didn't confirm or deny, but she knew. And what you are saying explains her curiosity."

My son and I had never discussed Ricky's affairs; there was no need. Ricky Brown was a legend in the city, and people talked. Chester knew what Ricky Brown was, and he knew I was his best friend.

"Her other questions make me think she already knew or suspected it."

Regina was in reporter mode. "What else did she ask you?" I was expecting her pen and note pad.

"How many kids he had, did I know them, what did they do, why did I call him uncle, had he been married before - stuff like that."

Regina said, "Yes, she knows. Those questions are about her siblings; she has none with Dr. Gates and his wife."

The phone on the kitchen wall rang. Chester got up to answer it. He pushed a button, and we all heard the tone. "They're back."

Ricky, Martha, and Angela entered happily laughing. Sonny came directly to me in the kitchen and sat next to my chair. I patted the back of his neck. Ricky walked to me too and said, "Well erbody know erdang naw. No mo' secrets."

"Good." Martha and Regina said in unison.

I looked at Angela, and her lips were smiling, but her eyes were not. Chester walked to her and wrapped his arms around her from the back.

"There is one more secret, and after tonight I am certain it should be shared." Angela stepped out of my son's embrace and turned to face him. "I am carrying Norton's child, not yours."

Chester nodded his head yes. "I know. He told me a month ago. I was waiting for you to tell me."

Angela started crying and my son stepped to her and wrapped his arms around her. They needed time alone. I stood and moved toward the door, and the others followed.

Chapter Fourteen

We took an Uber to my house, and the driver's Honda Accord's door wasn't closed before Regina said, "We raised a great son, and he is too good for that pothead. They can't get married. She was going to deceive him."

Sonny ran up the stairs ahead of us. I didn't respond to Regina and walked up the front porch steps. I was pushing my entry numbers into the keypad.

"Had she not gone through her emotional epiphany with Ricky and Martha, she would have deceived our son into marrying her. She has to go!" Regina was right behind me spewing venom against Angela. I understood her anger, partially, but I felt myself smiling.

"She is Ricky's daughter," I said.

"And what is that supposed to mean?" She hissed.

We were in the house. I closed the door and turned the deadbolt. I went to my chair and dropped in it. I leaned back, causing the recliner to extend the footrest. I picked up the remote and answered Regina's question with a "Nothing," but my nothing meant Angela was family, and I would give her the benefit of the doubt. I added, "She loves Chester," to my nothing.

Regina huffed, kicking off her shoes and sitting down on the couch. "No. Love is not on the table. She is looking for a 'baby daddy' since hers is dead."

I pushed the television on and turned to MSNBC. "That's not true. She is an accomplished young lady, and she has her own money. They are in love. Our son knew the baby was not his... that says a lot."

Regina sat back into a corner of the couch and looked up at the screen. "Our son is in lust, and that woman is on the hunt. We should have stayed and seen how the conversation turned out."

My couch was designed with only one long cushion, and most people got comfortable right away. Regina was settled with her feet up on the cushion. I told her, "What they decide is not our business. I think we know too much already."

Without taking her eyes from the news she said, "You would."

Her tone was snide, and the phrase was pregnant as hell. I started to cut the television off, but I didn't. I asked my ex-wife, "What is that supposed to mean?"

She looked from the television to me and said, "That means you like sticking your head in the sand and acting like everything is fine when the shit is about to hit the fan. That... is what I mean. Our son needs you to advise him against marrying that girl. Not to accept her because she is of Ricky's blood line. Your reasoning is insane!"

Her breathing got rapid, and her anger was real.

"This situation will not work itself out. You need to do something. For once, tell your son right from wrong. Damn, be a man and advise your son!" She was close to screaming and her ears were turning red.

"The baby Angela is carrying will be brain damaged from the amount of marijuana she is smoking. You want your son burdened with an addict wife and a special needs child? Do you?" She lowered the volume of her words, but her whole face and neck were red. She was overreacting, and I knew it, but telling her that would not have gone anywhere. I hadn't seen Regina that angry in decades.

There was a time when she was prone to explode if things didn't go her way, but I thought she had outgrown that type of childish anger. However, the look on her face told me different. She was angry at me because she wanted me to talk against Angela to Chester, and that was not going to happen. I cut off the television.

When we were married, if I didn't conform to what she wanted when she wanted, or if I seriously disagreed with her, she attacked me. I had assumed that part of her personality had fizzled away with age, but her words told me different. Her verbal attack was a habitual reflex, one that occurred when I didn't do what she wanted.

Sonny, who was laid next to my chair, sat up in response to her tone. He looked at her curiously then he looked at me. I commanded him to return to laying down, which he did.

"Regina, what I want is for my adult son to be happy. I want my college graduate, RN son, to manage his own life without my or your interference. I will not advise him contrary to his obvious desires. He knew Angela was carrying Norton's child, so he was not deceived. He was merely waiting on her to tell him the truth. He was moving at his pace."

She slung her feet to the floor and stood. "David! She slept with both of them. Norton and our son - she slept with two friends. Got pregnant by one and was willing to marry the other one. Shit, she is a slut!"

Regina went to the bar and poured herself a double shot of Gran Patron into a brandy snifter. She downed it in two gulps. She added ice to the snifter and poured another double; this one she sipped while looking at me.

Responding was not wise and I knew it, but I heard myself saying, "We don't know what their plans are. We know they both loved Norton, and that they will both love that child. You are screaming marriage. They have not said one word about marriage.

"Why Chester went along with her deception is beyond my understanding. Maybe because they both were grieving the loss of Norton. I don't know. But I do know what is not... my fuckin' business. That grown man's relationship with the person of his choice is not my damn business. Good night."

I stood from my chair and walked toward the steps. Sonny stood and jumped up on the couch and hung his head over the cushion, which was how he slept. Regina continued to sip her tequila looking at Sonny instead of me. I went up the stairs to my bedroom, not extending her an invite. Where she slept was not my concern.

She ordered Sonny to "Get off the couch, mutt." I heard him jumping to the floor and the television cutting back on.

*

I woke to the smell of bacon, coffee, and buttered toast. I showered and went down to the kitchen in my robe and house shoes. On the table was a full platter of bacon, a big bowl of scrambled eggs, a saucer with a tall stack of buttered toast, and a full pitcher of orange juice. It was close to my favorite breakfast; the only thing missing was cheese grits. Regina couldn't cook a pot of grits to save her life. I heard Sonny barking playfully in the backyard.

Regina was sitting at the head of the table butt naked with her chair pushed back and her thighs gapped wider than the chair she was sitting on. She was fingering her clitoris.

"You have to decide which meal to eat first. You can only get both if you choose wisely."

Again, I was angry at her, and I desired her.

I thought about her red face the night before. I thought about her mean words and her accusations. I thought about her stating what I didn't do for my son. So, I sat at the table and fixed my plate.

I thought she would have stopped playing with herself, but she didn't. She kept at it until I heard her pussy smacking with wetness. I tried to ignore her, but she started moaning then she said, "Get over here, D., and come put your damn tongue where it belongs."

I am certain a stronger man would have continued eating his bacon and eggs... but I dropped my fork and went to her. I put my face between her thighs until her knees locked on my ears. I stood picking her up, and she hung her legs over my shoulders. With my hands under her butt, I slide her down onto my hard jones. We were joined and standing. Her eyes were closed, and she was biting down on her bottom lip. I carried up the stairs to my bed with my jones inside her.

*

We didn't leave the house or answer a phone for two days. We sent the necessary text and nothing more. We didn't dress, we stayed naked, and we kept fucking. On the third day, I really didn't care about how she had looked at Lee or her thinking my head was in the sand. I was with the most beautiful woman in the world, and everything was right in the universe. But sadly, my satisfaction was temporary.

The evening of day three, I thought about her words concerning my parenting of Chester and how hateful her tone was. Despite being physically happy and relaxed, my mind grabbed ahold of the anger from argument. We were laying naked in the bed sharing a pillow, and I was physically satisfied, but my damn thinking drifted down a confrontational path.

I did not want to be on that path, so I decided to discuss my thoughts with her instead of letting them fester in my mind.

"Baby, we need to talk."

In response to my words, she wrapped her fingers around my jones and said, "No, we don't," and she started stroking it with her hand, and then she lowered her mouth to it. Regina and my jones were against talking.

An hour or so later, on the same pillow, I didn't tell her we needed to talk, I just started talking because the discussion was important to me.

"You have anger issues, and you are spoiled." I wasn't smiling when I said the words, and I didn't move my eyes from hers.

She kissed me on the lips and said, "Yes, and you keep spoiling me." She wasn't smiling either.

We were talking.

I did spoil her. I gave in to her wants most times because when she got her way, she was happy. My heart warmed when she smiled, and the things she wanted were usually of little consequence to me: movie choices, concerts choices, restaurant choices; but dating choices were different than life actions. Our life action choices were in conflict. I was not going to tell my grown son who he should date.

She put her fingertips on my cheek and caressed it. "You have issues too, D. You don't challenge people enough. You don't assert your will and wants onto others. You go along to get along, and that irritates me beyond belief."

I first reaction was to get defensive, but her words made me think, and I decided she was right. I try my best not to impose my will or my wants onto others. I prefer to be around people who want what I want. People who are not children know what they want.

I told her, "You are right. I don't want to make anybody do anything. Human relationships are not about domination. Forcing my will and my wants on others is not how I live my life."

Neither of us moved off the pillow, and neither of us was smiling.

She looked like she was about get up from the pillow, so I kissed her. She stayed on the pillow.

"The world works the opposite, D. You must know that; people get power by making others to do what they want. Control yields power. When people do what I want them to do, follow my thoughts, my wants, my desires, they are better off. I am not dominating them. I am directing them; my way is best."

Her lips smiled, but I knew damn well she was serious. She totally believed what she said.

"My mother told me you were infatuated with me, and that you would make a terrible husband. She said you were mesmerized by my looks and had placed me on a pedestal. I thought that was what a husband was supposed to do, so I married you."

She kissed me and looked directly into my eyes without blinking and said, "I don't think we should get married," and then she kissed me again.

After two and a half days of fucking each other silly, I honestly answered, "Me neither," and I kissed her, and I was so relieved. I loved her, and there was no denying that, but I did not want to marry her or live with her.

Regina had changed, but a lot of the old Regina was still present, and I didn't want that stress in my life. We had fundamentally different beliefs. She wanted others to succumb to her plans and directives. She felt she should lead others in relationships, and I didn't want to be led, by her or anyone else, and I didn't want to lead anyone. It was hard enough deciding what was best for me.

I had wants, goals, and desires of my own that required my full attention. I didn't have the time or the desire to be constantly battling, to be rebelling against being lead in a relationship. My life was about my goals and my desires. It was not about what someone else thought I should be doing.

Regina added, "But I still want to go to Barbados with you," and she kissed me again.

"Me too," and I did want to go with her because a vacation was not a life commitment.

We kissed and smiled at each other.

Regina said, "I want a steak."

"The Chop House?" I asked.

"Yes," she answered.

*

We were dressed and ready to go out to dinner. The doorbell rang when I was in the kitchen. Regina and Sonny both went to the door. Regina yelled from the door, "It's your business partner."

I heard the door opening and I heard Carol saying, "You two must not know. Do you? Turn on the television."

Whatever it was, I didn't want to know. The outside world was fine outside. Sonny came into the kitchen and Carol and Regina remained the living area. Sonny looked up at me then looked to the living area and then back at me. I heard the television.

"Both detectives were veterans of the force with stellar records."

I slowly entered the living area with Sonny at my side. Carol and Regina were both standing in front of the fifty-inch television. On the screen were photos of Lee and Dixon.

"The detectives were gunned down execution style in front of the library at 35th and King Drive." There was no reporter on the screen, just the detective's photos. The scene switched to a shot of the library with a very pretty Black reporter standing in front of the building.

"He was getting married next month," Regina said. "I should call April, his fiancé. I introduced them." She had the television remote in her hand. She pointed it at the television and cut it off.

That surprised me.

I asked Carol, "What do you know?"

"Like Regina said, April Johnson, the head librarian, was Lee's fiancé. He was there to see her. Lee parked, and both detectives got out of the car and walked toward the library. Witnesses say three men walked up on them and opened fire, all head shots. Lee and Dixon died instantly."

"When?" Regina asked, standing in front of and looking at the black screen.

"About four hours ago."

"Who were the witnesses?" I asked.

"Patrons exiting the library. The shooters only shot Detectives Lee and Dixon. One of the witnesses says a black sedan pulled up after the shooting, and the three calmly got in and left."

Regina released a lengthy exhale and walked to the couch and sat. "Who kills police detectives, guns them down in the middle of the day?" She looked to me and to Carol.

"Any descriptions on the shooters?" I asked Carol.

"Black nylon ski masks with black pistols. Dark colored clothes, but no real descriptions. People were scared and trying to get to safety."

I went to my chair and sat, and Carol sat on the couch next to Regina. Sonny laid next to my chair. We sat for a few quiet moments until Ricky called my cell.

"I know y'all on lock down and over dere fuckin' like bunnies, but did cha hear 'bout Gina's boyfriend?"

I didn't correct him. I just answered, "Yeah, Carol is here updating us now."

"One of 'dem had to be involved in some shit ta get shot down like dat or maybe both of dem."

"Yeah, looks like it."

"If I was you, I would stay far away from dis shit. Don't let Gina talk ya into some stupid shit. Let da police handle dis mess."

The other line beeped, and I saw Langston Waters' name and number on my screen.

"Hold on, Ricky." I clicked over.

"Mr. Price, my aunt called me with the news. What do you think happened with my cousin?"

I never thought about Detective Lee having a mother.

Waters continued with, "I would like to hire you to look into Johnny's murder."

I didn't hesitate to say, "Mr. Waters, I am not a detective."

Regina suddenly stood from the couch nodding her head yes. "Take the case," she mouthed.

Carol was also nodded her head yes and whispered, "He pays well and right away."

I was not feeling the case, and Ricky's words were echoing in my mind. Investigating murdered police officers was way beyond what I did. Both Carol and Regina walked over to me, so I put Waters on speaker, allowing them to hear him.

"Mr. Waters, I run a protection service, not a detective agency." I was informing him, Regina, and Carol.

"Yes, but you have investigative skills, and as before, I would like to hire you to protect me while we probe into the case."

I shook my head no and told him, "Mr. Waters, you being former military police does not make you a detective either."

"I agree in part, but my cousin was murdered, and I was military police and that experience allowed me a skillset that I am sure will produce some answers. Protect me while I snoop around… that is all I am asking."

Both Regina and Carol were looking at me as if my acceptance was an obvious yes.

Waters said, "I will double your fee."

Carol's hands went up and Regina's eyebrows rose. The two most important women in my life were in agreement, so I said, "I will agree to five days."

Both women smiled, showing their very white teeth.

"Thank you, Mr. Price. I will be back in Chicago day after tomorrow. See you then."

We disconnected the call. Regina and Carol placed their hands on my shoulders. I switched back to Ricky.

"Ya got talked inta it, didn't ya?"

"I did."

"Ok, so ya fidna look inta one dead cop?"

"So it seems."

The End

Made in the USA
Middletown, DE
06 January 2023

18595189R00130